Travis I. Sivart

Eye in the Sky

The Traveller's Inn, Book 3

Travis I. Sivart

Travis I. Sivart

Eye in the Sky

The Traveller's Inn, Book 3

Talk of the Tavern Publishing Group

Table of Contents

1. Taking Off

Kitty ran her hand through her short, spiky pink hair and eyed Durg. She knew she could take him. She might only come up to his nipples, and he might be able to bench press a plow horse, but she was quick and knew the points to hit a person to take them down. Durg watched her with dull eyes, a childish grin on his face. He looked innocent, like a toddler, but she didn't care. Toddlers were trouble, everyone knew that. The moron had looked at her, and that was enough for her to call him out.

"Kitty," Croaker said, placing a hand on her shoulder, "he did nothing. Only laughed when you did. Stop being so angry. It only poisons you. It'll lead to a short—and unhappy—life if you can't get past it."

She tensed under her friend's grip, wanting to grab his gnarled hand, bend it backwards, and break a few fingers. With a twist of his wrist, Croaker would be on his knees and the perfect height to land a roundhouse kick on the side of his head.

The rest of the Traveller's Inn had gone quiet, watching the confrontation at the bar. The place looked different than it had before, but Kitty couldn't quite put a finger on what changed. It was decorated with sleek, dark vinyl furniture, neon trimming the edge of the ceiling and the step up to the booths ringing the room. Industrial metal pipes and venting showed in the open ceiling, and the dull thrum of techno music vibrated from hidden speakers.

The regulars were scattered around the room. Nomed and Wanderly shared their customary booth, the first with a rye on the rocks, the smaller man with something bright red and a small fruit salad bursting over the rim. Nomed's handsome face had a tight smile as he straightened the thin black tie over his shiny silver shirt. Wanderly tousled his own curly hair, and Kitty thought he must be in the middle of a story, and oblivious to the showdown. But Wanderly was never oblivious.

Darome, Durg's partner and boss, stood on a barstool and still wasn't as tall as Kitty, who was a slight woman to begin with. He wore his usual purple zoot suit, and fiddled with a fat, gold ring on his finger. The tiny man watched her, his usual smile gone. She couldn't tell if he was afraid, angry, or just waiting.

Why does he feel the need to protect his gigantic goon? She thought.

"Miss Kitty, if I may offer another solution to this standoff?" Drawled Cogsley, the dapper barman and Maître d'. He kowtowed to everyone, but only bowed to Jack Tucker, the proprietor of the place. "Perhaps I can offer a drink instead of a tussle. The place was just renovated, and I would hate to see you damage the upgrades on its first day. May I suggest a rum runner or a hurricane? Both are blended with a wonderful helping of spirits to soothe and cool."

"Frag off, chrome dome," she muttered to Cogsley, then shook Croaker's hand from her shoulder. "I'll fight when I feel like it."

"And do you feel like it right now?" Croaker asked, taking a step back. "Right when Jack is offering you your first job for him and the Traveller's Inn? It seems like bad timing, kid. Might even be a bit of that self-destructive urge we've talked about kicking in."

Croaker was the only one she let talk to her like this. He was older and had seen his share of shit in life. Most of it kicked in his face or fed to him by others using a huge spoon. He'd become family to her, a sort of Dutch uncle that had adopted her. But he never *told* her what to do. Just suggested and pointed out what she might be feeling.

"Fine," Kitty spat, "whatever. I'll let it slide this time. But Darome, you keep your dog on a leash and on his side of the yard. You read me?"

"Wuff, wuff," Durg grunted, grinning and turning to Darome. "Imma puppy, Darome. Didn't I sound just like a puppy?"

"Yeah, sure Durg," Darome nodded, watching Kitty take two steps back and turn away. "Come on over here and I'll scratch behind your ear and get you a treat. Want some steak fries with gravy? Does that sound good?"

"Idiots," Kitty muttered, pushing past Croaker and going to her regular seat at the other end of the bar. Pulling herself onto the stool, she grabbed a handful of pretzels and looked at Croaker. "Why do they let them in here? They're useless."

"They have their uses," a voice said from behind her where no one had been a moment before.

Spinning around, vibro-knife in her hand, Kitty saw Jack leaning on the end of the bar, a small smile playing across his lips. He looked from her scowl to the blade and back up again.

"Never even saw you draw it," Jack said admiringly. "Wow, you're almost quicker than anyone I know. Maybe even faster than Nomed."

The murmur of the tavern picked up as Kitty bristled and preened under the compliment at the same time. There were only a dozen or so people in the place, and it never seemed to get busy enough in Kitty's mind to justify the expense of the business. Jack never seemed bothered by the lack of customers. She wondered if he was some sort of rich eccentric, redecorating the entire theme of the place on a whim. She'd seen it as an old English pub, a country western saloon, and now as the sleek punk club. But she'd never seen it closed. It's like the entire place changed in the blink of an eye by magic or something.

She studied Jack. He wore his usual outfit. A white button-up shirt, slightly wrinkled, khaki slacks, also wrinkled, and a bemused but piercingly intelligent look on his face. His hair wasn't short but didn't reach his collar, and was the nondescript color you saw everywhere and never noticed. He was of medium height, not short nor tall and his eyes were-

"So," Jack broke into her thoughts, speaking to her and Croaker, "you ready for this?"

Looking back at Croaker, Kitty saw the older man had retrieved his brown canvas duster and beaten fedora. He rubbed at the stubble on his leathery cheeks and lifted his whiskey with an arthritic hand. Croaker raised it in a toast and threw back the drink in three long swallows.

"Flask filled," Croaker said, gasping slightly at the burn of the liquor, "six-shooter on my hip, and my bag has a bunch of gadgets and gizmos that may come in handy. I'm ready."

"What's the job?" Kitty asked, glancing down at her outfit and wondering if it was right for the work she'd agreed to do.

She wore a leather harness over a sleeveless, pale rose muscle shirt, and black cargo pants. The harness could accommodate anything from a shoulder holster, to pouches, to, well, anything she wanted to clip to the various mismatched d-rings. Of course, Kitty would never carry or use a gun. She had a deep-seated loathing of the things. If she were going to maim or kill someone, she wanted to do it up close and personal with her knife or vibro-whip.

"I'm sending you to Fort Managogic, Iowa," Jack explained, "to find a scientist and professor named Dr. Emmet San Guglielmo. He works at the University of Fort

Managogic and has been doing wonderful work with a small hadron collider, mixing the proton collisions with electrical pulses with the strength of lightning strikes. He may have stumbled onto a mixture that crosses certain…boundaries."

Jack paused, and Kitty wasn't sure if he was waiting for questions or being dramatic.

"Sounds great," Croaker interjected, "and who did you get for our team? You usually gather everyone in the Traveller's Inn and send them all out together. Are they here yet?"

"No, no, no," Jack laughed. "You're like a kid at Christmas, Croaker. I haven't seen you this excited in a long time. Not since North Mirron. But I've contacted Byron Savage. I think you know him."

"That madman?" Croaker choked. He tapped his glass and threw a glance at Cogsley, indicting he'd need another drink for this.

Kitty stiffened at his reaction as the man went on.

"He might be a top-notch bounty hunter, but he ain't right in the head. Silver told me about him. Mixed up moral code bordering on god-complex. Overpowered implants that might be tracked by the T.A.L.O.N. Agency, and a list of enemies the length of my pecker. And trust me, it's not as long as it used to be, but it's still respectable!"

"Croaker," Kitty sighed fondly and rolled her eyes, "you're so last century, you patriarchal, misogynistic asshole. Let the man finish, and we can mock your wrinkly manhood afterwards."

"I also brought in Jamie Erich, who prefers to go by the Haunt," Jack continued, "a man who is a psychic medium. The last person on your team may be the most impressive. He'll be your face man, the one who has all the contacts and can get you what you need when you need something no one else can get. His name is, and don't laugh, Fritz Spitz."

Kitty laughed, a short braying bark, then slapped her hand over her mouth.

"That's your one time, Kitty," Jack said, smiling but with

serious eyes. "Don't laugh at this man. He can be a bit sensitive, but he's great at what he does. A winning personality that draws people to him and makes folks trust him. And in a pinch, he's not bad in a fight."

"Great, okay," Kitty said around her blunted snickering. "So, when do we leave?"

"Right now," Jack said, gesturing towards an emergency exit in the rear of the room Kitty hadn't noticed before, "if you're both ready. I have a plane waiting to drop you, and you'll be there before you know it."

"Great," Kitty said, sliding off her stool and dropping to the floor.

"Yeah, okay," Croaker said slowly, standing up, "it's not going to be like that time-"

"Nothing like that time, Croaker, I promise," Jack interrupted, holding up his hands. The proprietor turned to lead the way to the exit, and muttered, "at least, not exactly like that time. Mostly."

Kitty saw the man's shoulders shaking as the trio crossed the empty dance floor and wondered what the two were talking about.

Jack stopped at the door, turning to face them with one hand on the push bar.

"You both ready?" he asked. "Move quick once I open it. Time flies, and so do other things."

"Jack..." Croaker growled menacingly as the man pushed open the door.

A blinding white light flooded into the room, bright as the noontime sun compared to the dim interior of the Traveller's Inn. Kitty stepped through, but heard the final exchange between Jack and Croaker.

"Jack," Croaker spat, "are you sending us into a-"

"Just get in there and handle things with your usual style and flair," Jack said, laughing jovially. "And you'll be fine. Oh, and the way back here mirrors the real world!"

Jack shrugged, looking around.

"I hope he heard that last part," he grinned. "Well, either

way, Croaker is a resourceful old coot. He'll figure it out."

Alarms blared.

Kitty stumbled, the metal plating shifting under her feet. The tube-like room angled down and to her right. The sound of turbine engines whined and the roar of fast-moving air tossed loose papers around her. Croaker plowed into her and they both went down into a heap.

"Jack, damn you!" Croaker roared. "This is to get back at me for that hovercycle fiasco, isn't it?"

"Shut up, old man," Kitty barked, standing up again, her arms held out on each side like a surfer catching the biggest wave of their life. "Where the frag are we?"

"In a plane," Croaker shouted over the wind, "that's going down."

The old man pushed to his feet, spreading them wide and duck walking until he reached the side of the cargo area, and grabbed the thick web netting used to secure crates and gear. He wobbled forward, hand over hand, his long coat flaring around him, heading down and toward where Kitty presumed the cockpit should be.

"But how'd we get into a plane?" Kitty tried to say calmly, but it came out more as an undisciplined, panicked screech.

"Jack has a knack," Croaker said, "for getting people places quicker than most people could imagine."

Kitty balanced on the balls of her feet, her antique Doc Martins giving her traction when other footwear would have slipped, and followed her mentor and friend towards his destination. He stopped at what looked more like an airlock than a door, spun the dial-like handle and muscled it open. Inside were two seats with w-shaped steering wheels. Both chairs were empty and twin holes, perfectly circular, were cut from the two-centimeter-thick glass in front of them. No one was in the pilot or copilot seats. The last edge of the sun sunk behind the horizon and the sky turned from crimson and orange to deep blues and purples.

2. Landing Gears

Fritz Spitz watched from a jump seat in the rear of the plane as the old man and the pink-haired tart popped into the door that the pilot and copilot had leapt out of moments before.

That's weird, Fritz thought. *I wonder if they were just waiting for the other guys to leave before coming in. I was wondering how they'd get here, considering we're at 27,000 feet.*

He'd been here since before takeoff, quietly boarding the small cargo plane—built in the previous century—and finding his way to the rear of the plane and a seat. Just like Jack had told him to do.

Jack said to find a plane that suits their needs, get on it, and wait. And that's what I did, because I'm good. Fritz thought, kicking his feet back and forth as the new people got their balance, then fell. *Jack will probably tell me that too and give me a reward for doing such a good job. I like Jack, and I believe in being loyal to those you like.*

He'd been on the plane since it took off from Cincinnati. They didn't even have snacks. He was hoping for snacks, but had brought some jerky along just in case no one else had anything. He'd napped a bit, until the odd lightning struck, and the two pilots fell all over one another, trying to abandon their seats and head for the side door. It had looked like fun, but Jack had told him to stay put and not do anything until Fritz's new team arrived. He'd watched the pilots fumble at the hatch and leap out. Then there had been another flare of odd light, and Croaker and Kitty had stumbled in.

Cocking his head and twitching his ears forward, Fritz studied the two making their way to the cabin. The rush of air from the cockpit pushed the scent of the two back to Fritz who took a big, long sniff.

Ugh, is he drunk? And he smells like batteries, gasoline, and oil. Fritz focused on the woman. *She smells like angst and bubblegum. Even more weird. Jack told me to expect these two, but he didn't tell me to expect this.*

Fritz unlatched his seat belt, dropped from the cushion to the floor, and padded towards the front. The slipstream in the fuselage blew his thick, russet hair back. Fritz opened his mouth, savoring the stream of wind as he moved forward, his tongue almost lolling out of his mouth.

"Do you know how to fly a plane?" Croaker and Kitty said simultaneously.

"Yeah." Croaker nodded, leaning over the captain's chair and studying the controls. He gripped the steering and leveled the plane off. "Probably. Mostly. I've flown a few things. How hard can it be to fly this old bucket?"

Fritz Spitz leaned to the side, looking past Kitty. She was only a little taller than him. Croaker was studying the control panel, running his fingers over the lights, dials, and other gizmos.

"Well, there's a lot of dials and switches," Fritz said, gazing up at them with amber eyes.

Croaker and Kitty turned and looked, then shifted their eyes down to see a short man with a russet pompadour hair style in a blown back look and inquisitive amber eyes. Fritz stared back up, grinning a toothy grin and his inquisitive eyes gleaming. He brushed at his military green flight suit and cocked his head up at them.

"Fritz Spitz, Jack sent me. But you knew that already, I bet, didn't you?" Fritz said and shoved his hand forward. "Shake?"

Kitty's hand crept forward, and Fritz shoved his hand into hers. He gave three quick pumps, then pulled his hand away and thrust it towards Croaker. "Shake?"

Croaker knitted his brow, scowling, and shook Fritz's proffered hand. Fritz gave three pumps, then withdrew a step.

"You're German?" Kitty asked, unable to come up with anything wittier.

"Yah," Fritz smiled at Kitty, "I am of German stock, but I think we should focus on landing and meeting the rest of the team before we do anything else. Jamie and Byron are at the field. Croaker, I got us the plane. You think you can fly it?"

"I can fly anything," Croaker muttered, turning and dropping into the captain's chair. Strapping in, he said, "This damn wind is annoying, though. What the hell happened? And how'd it cut perfect twin circles in glass that thick?"

"I dunno," Fritz shrugged, leaning into the passing current of air, "some sort of freak lightning. It scared the hell out of the two men in here, and they jumped out of the plane right before you stumbled in."

"But how did we jump into a plane thousands of meters feet off the ground?" Kitty asked.

"Doesn't matter," Croaker growled. "Sit down and help me keep her level. Anyone know how far it is to Fort Managogic?"

"About 27,000 feet, straight down, would be my guess," Fritz shrugged, holding onto the handle outside of the cockpit and leaning in, swinging back and forth and biting at the column of air shooting past. "Because I think we should be right above it. So, you get the easy part. You only need to land the plane."

"Easy part?" Croaker said, without looking back.

"Takeoff and landing are the hard parts. Flying in a straight line is the easy part. And this thing is around a hundred years old, so pre-computers, meaning I'll have to land it without assistance."

"You told me you hate computers anyway," Kitty said, strapping into the copilot's seat. "You said they're pushy and going to kill everyone someday."

"And I still stand by that," Croaker huffed, gripping the wheel with both hands. "But when dropping from the sky, I wouldn't say no to some help."

"Glad to hear that," Fritz said in a relieved tone. "About hating computers, that is. Because I'm pretty sure that the electrical pulse—whatever it was—fried any retrofitted computers and electronics in this tub. Only thing remaining is the old-fashioned mechanical instruments."

"I'm okay with that," Croaker said distractedly, checking the dials. "Now, stop yapping at me so I can get us down without killing us."

Fritz spun around the corner and hopped up onto the jump seat behind the cockpit and buckled in. He listened to Croaker swear under his breath.

Jack had told Fritz about these two, just a little, but the little man was able to sniff out a bit more about them in the short time he'd known them. Croaker reminded Fritz of his dear ol' grandad. He was gruff and would cuff you as soon as look at you, but he knew his stuff. Grandad was also loyal to a fault, and once you had him in your corner, he'd hang onto you like a dog with a bone. He might growl, but it was done with love. Fritz figured Croaker was the same way. He just put on a show to keep folks at arm's length, so he never needed to show his actual feelings.

Kitty was feisty and sassy. She'd hiss and spit, staying aloof and distant, never letting anyone know her true feelings—*Maybe that's why the two of them get along so well*, Fritz thought, *because they're so alike, but so different*—all the while acting like she was queen of the castle.

The airplane shifted, banking to the left and nosing

downward in a gentle curve. It jittered through some turbulence and Fritz let out a small bark of surprise, then laughed.

"There's a beacon on the landing strip," Fritz shouted over the wind, "and landing in the twilight should offer some cover. Just don't crash!"

"You're not helping," growled Croaker.

"The part of about the beacon was helpful," Kitty chimed in.

"Don't defend the runt," Croaker muttered, and the plane banked again.

Fritz smashed against the side of the plane and the cargo in the fuselage's rear caught his attention. A dozen large crates taller than most men shifted in the thick webbing strapping them to the deck.

"I wonder what they have in them," Fritz murmured to no one in particular, unbuckling and dropping to the floor. "You'd think I'd have checked them while sitting back there, but nappies sounded good. Something about being in a moving vehicle makes me want to nap."

He padded the length of the plane, sticking to the wall and avoiding the open door on the other side. Reaching the seat he'd been in originally, he leaned down and picked up his forgotten backpack. Slinging it over one arm, then the other, he studied the cargo, looking for markings.

"Maybe they have a bill of lading or something," Fritz said, stumbling forward to grab the cargo netting. "Of course, it's probably done digitally, like everything else nowadays. Just scan a code and the info comes up if you have the right app."

Moving along the double row of crates, he stopped. There was something spray painted on the back side of the third crate, between it and the next one. There was a thin space between the two, and Fritz eyed it.

"I should be able to squeeze into that space," he muttered, "and then use my cardphone's flashlight to read it. Yeah, that should work."

He did just that, wiggling into the space and shimmying along, wooden splinters catching at his flight suit and pulling at his sleeves. He had to stop and take his backpack off so he could move in further. Holding it in one hand, he wiggled further in.

"That should be far enough," he said happily, and held up his wrist where his cardphone was secured to the bracer he wore. "Um, can't get my other hand up there to…"

He dropped the backpack and raised his now free hand over his head. He tried to work his arm around his noggin to press the light on the phone.

"Can't reach," he sighed. "What if I…"

He raised the other arm, the one with the cardphone, bringing to closer to his free hand, fingers wiggling as he tried to touch his phone. The two hands met, and he giggled in triumph. Turning his head up, he tried to see where to press to turn on the flashlight, fumbling around.

The plane jumped again as it hit turbulence, and the crates shifted. They slid apart, just a few centimeters, but it was enough for him to bring both hands in front of his face and press the light icon.

The thin alley between the massive wooden boxes flooded with a bright, white illumination and Fritz blinked in the sudden glare.

"Buckle up and hold on," Croaker shouted from the cockpit, "we're about to land and it might knock things around a bit!"

"Uh oh," Fritz said, considering his options. "Play it safe and get out of here? Or let my eyes adjust, see what's on the crate, and then get out of here?"

He looked up towards the markings and straight into the light.

"Dammit," he sputtered, turning his wrist so the light bathed the side of the massive box, and blinked his eyes rapidly to clear the light blindness.

Glancing up again, he saw the blurry outline of words and a symbol as large as his head. The plane struck the tarmac with a squealing hop and the crates shifted further apart, allowing Fritz to look up and focus on the script and pictograph.

The plane bounced again, and the crates scraped closer to one another. Fritz felt the thick wood press against his back, trapping his arm between his neck and the other crate. With a yelp, he began shuffling to the side, rushing to get out from between the massive boxes. One bad bounce and he'd be pâté. Literal dog food.

The plane touched down for the third and final time, causing the boxes to move apart again. Fritz tumbled to the deck, sprawling over his backpack as the crates freed him.

"I'll be a son of a bitch," he growled, throwing the backpack at the wall where it tumbled down the curve of the fuselage and came to rest on the floor.

The plane taxied down the runaway, slowing in jerks and shudders as Croaker tried to stop the unfamiliar craft. The crates jittered and shimmied, closing the gap between the two in grinding scrapes and thudding bumps.

Fritz crawled frantically towards the end of the shrinking hallway, pulling himself along with his fingers in the deck plating. The boxes squeezed his shoulders and Fritz flipped onto his side, dragging himself by his fingernails towards the fast-dwindling gap at the end of his personal chasm of death.

Fingertips grasping the edge of the crate, he sucked in his stomach and let out his breath to make himself as slim as humanly possible. He pulled, shooting bodily out of the wooden canyon as the plane stopped with a jerk and the crates slammed together.

Fritz lay on his back, knees curled to his belly and feet pressed to the crates, panting. Croaker and Kitty came out of the cockpit and caught sight of him.

"Come on," Croaker spat, "quit lounging around like a hound dog sunning himself on the porch. We've got things to do."

"Yeah," Kitty hissed, "and why are you breathing so

heavy. It's not like you were doing anything strenuous or stressful. Dumbass."

Fritz whimpered, watching the two move to the open hatch on the side of the plane, the same one they'd come through not too long ago, and disappear into the early night.

3. Testing the Waters

Jamie "the Goddamned Haunt" Erich watched the old man and the young chickie climb down from the open door in the side of the plane. He felt calm below the surface of a polluted sheen, driven by intellect but a churning cesspool of regret and guilt. The old man reminded Jamie of his Pawpaw, right down to the glare and sneer.

If he walks up and smacks me in the side of the head, Jamie thought, *I might begin to think I've just found my Pawpaw's brother.*

The girlie-girl though, she was a hottie with bright pink hair, tight pants, and a thin, athletic build that made Jamie sit up and notice, in more than one way. The vibe coming off her was the urge to prove herself by beating down anyone who questioned or doubted her.

Is that a hand cannon I spy with my little eye? Jamie wondered, staring at the woman's forearm, which ended in a chromed muzzle as wide as her dainty wrist. *How'd she get her arms so toned when missing a hand? You can't do a chin up with that thing. You'd risk putting a hole in the ceiling!*

Rain fell, and a slow rumble in the west promised the weather would intensify before the night was through. The droplets spattered around Jamie, but never directly on him. He'd never allow that, not with his silk suit and wool overcoat. He adjusted his homburg hat, tilted the curved rim at a jaunty angle.

A small man with finger-length, swept back, orangey-brown hair appeared in the plane's doorway. Jamie's other sense tingled with the shadow of the supernatural pouring off this harmless-looking chap. He turned his face towards the clouds, sniffing and giving a little shake.

He's got a dark side. I can feel it. And does he sense something? Jamie titled his head. *Is he like me? Can he smell things other people can't?*

"Come on, kid," Byron Savage said from behind him. His voice was like rocks in a tumbler. "Stop gawking and get a move on."

The bounty hunter bumped Jamie's shoulder as he brushed past.

"Rude," Jamie muttered at the unnecessary contact, "we're on a goddamned runway, plenty of room to go around."

"You say something?" Savage said, stopping and turning to look at Jamie. "You can say it louder if you want. Uppity little punks like you are allowed to voice their opinions, you know that, right? You're just more likely to eat a fist for being an asshole, but that's okay. I'm all about taking advantage of a learning opportunity."

"Everything okay here?" Croaker asked, stepping in front of the two men.

"Fine," Savage turned a wooden grin on the older man, "just having a discussion about sharing with Jamie here."

"Yeah," Jamie nodded, putting on a suave air, "the tin man is merely showing his mettle, if you get the pun. His type always needs to use their brutish nature to-"

"Enough," Croaker barked. "I'm in charge of the mission, and we've got things to do. If you two want to compare cock sizes, do it after we finish the job."

"You worked with Silver and Smith, right?" Savage squared up in front of the older man, looming over him. "You got them the job where I ran into them, if I remember right."

"Sure, that's me," Croaker nodded, squinting up from under his beat up fedora, "and you're the top-notch bounty hunter that no one wants to touch. Is it because of who's hunting you, or your natural charm?"

Jamie snickered and Croaker turned to him.

"Wouldn't laugh too much, Haunt," Croaker said, the two looking like they had the same fashion taste but one from the high-end stores, the other from second-hand shops. "You've had some trouble, also, and though you've made yourself rich, it's been done through other people's troubles. Plus, I'm pretty sure some folks are looking for you, too. The same ones Savage here is avoiding. You two have more in common than you'd care to admit."

"He smells like perfume and seafood," Fritz said from Croaker's elbow, "like he's covering something. Could be the smell of the streets. That's where he comes from, right?"

"Doesn't matter," Croaker held up a hand, stopping Jamie from replying. "Look here, we're all misfits. Losers and outcasts. But that doesn't mean we don't have skills and won't wreck someone's day."

He took a step back, raising his arms to include everyone.

"I'm a planner and see opportunities most people miss, plus I can use almost any tech, or build it from a tin can and bubble gum if we don't have any. Kitty here has a bad temper and a quick reaction with her hand cannon, literally, or vibro-knife or vibro-whip. Fritz can sniff out anything we need in a moment's notice, from gear to food to hotels to weird shit. Savage, you're raw muscle and tech. You're the tank in a ring of small firearms. And Haunt, you're very special. You can see the things that go bump in the night. You can touch people—physically, mentally, or emotionally—without ever using a hand. Did I miss anything?"

The other four looked around at one another.

"Yeah," Kitty said, glaring at Jamie, "why isn't the rain

touching that guy? And when is he going to stop staring at my tits?"

"See?" Croaker grinned, then spat. "He's already influencing people and things around him. Now, if there's nothing else, we have a scientist to meet. Here's what you need to know about him…"

The others looked at Croaker expectantly.

"He's prompt," Croaker ticked off one finger, then pointed into the distance with it, "and he's pulling up right now."

Twin beams of headlights cut through the drizzle as an electric vehicle hummed towards the small group. The minivan came into focus in the misting weather and pulled up alongside them. The passenger window whirred down and a middle-aged man looked out, his white hair wild. It flared around his head and danced in the breeze.

"Greetings Earthlings," the driver said, holding up an ID badge from Fort Managogic University, "I'm Professor Emmet San Guglielmo, PhD and I'm here to share the wonders of the quantum multiverse, the terrors that lurk beyond, and the reality hovering over and under ours!"

"Dramatic much?" Kitty mumbled.

"His head is a mess," Jamie winced. "Doesn't he know what a stylist is, or at least own a comb?"

"He smells like cheese," Fritz chimed in, sounding excited.

"I love cheese," the Professor-Doctor crowed, equally excited. "Just had some. Have another couple bricks in my cooler if you'd like some."

"And he has a dry minivan," Savage added, pushing past the others and rolling the side door open. "I get the back seat. Alone."

Croaker opened the passenger door and slid in as Kitty, Fritz, and Jamie piled into the middle.

Jamie stared at the driver as the door whirred closed and the minivan took a wide U-turn and accelerated back the way it had come. He wrinkled his brow, watching the

Doctor-Professor as he tuned into his other sense, the one that made him a shit-ton of money. The man felt like a thunderstorm sweeping in from clear skies, casting a thick pall across Jamie's perception.

"Welcome to Iowa, America's heartland," the man said, gesturing to the landscape whipping past with both hands, "though some call this America's Dark Heartland because of the shadowy past, as well as what we've only recently discovered."

"And what exactly did you discover, Doctor, um, Professor…" Croaker trailed off as they took a sharp turn out of the small airport and onto the main road.

"Oh, you can call me Doctor, Professor, Emmet, or just Elmo, which is a nickname derived from my last name of San Guglielmo. And before I tell you what is going on in the present, allow me to tell you some of the fascinating and very true history first."

Jamie *felt* the scent of sulphur and ozone on the man, and wondered if it was a real smell or just his abilities picking up on something. Either way, it could be something mundane from the man's work. He looked away and into the tall field of crops beside the road they sped along.

"The township of Fort Managogic," Elmo continued, "was established on the fifth meridian, or principle, and the 42nd parallel. It was built on the Meskwaki Nation's lands, after the French and other white settlers chased the native people south to Missouri in the early 1800s. Oh, fun fact, the French called the Meskwaki people the Renard, or Fox, tribe because they were crafty and the encroaching pioneers swore they used magic. Originally named Fort Madison, it was changed when these incredible ruins were discovered."

"And was there magic?" Jamie asked, sliding into Fritz on the bench seat as the vehicle swerved into the traffic on Route 61, trying to get the man to open up to his sixth sense. "Either in the land or the displaced people?"

"I think there was," Elmo nodded, waving excitedly. "The University, which we're headed to, was built about thirty years ago. When excavating the underground tunnels for the small hadron collider, the construction crews found a series of stone underground structures, which dated back to the beginning of the Gregorian calendar."

"When the calendar was put into use, or when it was retroactively set to start?" asked Fritz, pushing Jamie back towards the window.

"Oh, great question!" Elmo crowed and threw his hands up. The minivan jigged into the passing lane and shot by an antique Tesla. "Definitely the latter. There're hundreds of underground rooms, all connected by a network of rounded tunnels large enough to walk upright in. When mapped with ground sonar, it showed a very interesting and significant pattern. A configuration long thought to focus arcane and otherworldly information by the ancient peoples all across the world. And the University of Fort Managogic was built in the very center of them. We even used the rooms and tunnels to lay down our circular tubes for the collider and other offshoot chambers. It's funny how science keeps reinventing the wheel that long extinct civilizations seemed to know about long before we were around."

"So, you think the underground complex," Croaker asked, gripping the dashboard with one hand and the oh-shit handle with the other, "and the shapes made by the chambers mean something?"

"Fun fact," Elmo said, flailing his arms as the minivan steered itself around a double-trailer cow transport, "in the language of the Meskwaki, Managogic means deep magic. Though some translate deep as shadow or lurking sort of waiting things, and magic as energies or consciousness. It's open to interpretation."

"That's some pretty fucking Lovecraftian and Cthulhu shit right there," Byron said from the back of the van, one arm braced on each window to stop himself from being thrown around, "and I'd know after what I dealt with in Peru."

Elmo slammed on the brakes and spun the steering

wheel, the minivan flying off the highway and onto an exit. It slid sideways a few meters, fishtailing until it got traction and shot forward.

"There's the Old Barn Taxidermy & Meat Processing, right beside the Fort Managogic Farm & Home Supply," Elmo tapped a thick, yellowed fingernail on the driver's side window. A wide, low building showed off the main road, a hunkered grey structure in the continuing downpour. Lightning cut through the sky, followed by an ominous rumble of thunder. "Oh, I've spent some money there, yes indeedy! I could tell you stories!"

Elmo laughed, a short, crisp throaty noise. "Anyhow, as I was saying, the college shut down to students about five years ago after a really weird accident and an incident with a serial killer, but they still let me use my grant money to use the facilities for my experiments. Very convenient to the Hy-Vee Grocery Store and other shops."

The vehicle careened into an empty parking lot, weaving between concrete islands of brown grass and skeletal trees stretching towards the murky clouds. Slamming on the brakes, he jerked the wheel hard, and the minivan spun into the parking space closest to the building.

"We're here," Elmo breathed, staring at the two-story brick and stucco building. Lightning flashed again, a sudden and sharp crash of thunder shaking the passengers within the vehicle.

4. Being Schooled

"Let me out of here!" Kitty surged towards the door release, slapping at it multiple times, spilling out of the minivan before the door had slid open completely. She landed on her hands and knees, heaving on the cracked asphalt with loud throaty noises.

"Is she okay?" Elmo asked, unbuckling his five-point safety harness and opening his door. "Some folks have been known to have reactions to the University. Vomiting is the least of them, but it is one of them."

"Yah," Fritz said, bounding out of the door and squatting beside Kitty, one hand on her spasming shoulder. "I tink she'll be fine. She just needs a moment."

"Don't…" Kitty growled, jerking, "touch…me."

"Yah," Fritz patted her, "I know, I know. But you don't have any hair to hold back, and I tink dat most people need some pats or pets when sicking up. You just worry about you, I gots you."

"Really," Croaker said, stepping around the two, "I wouldn't touch her. She gets pretty sensitive about that kind of thing."

Byron got out the driver's side door, following Jamie, who ran for the shelter of the building. The bounty hunter scanned the rooftop of the University for movement or figures. He listened to the street samurai being comforted by the odd little man and smiled. He remembered having friends who would comfort him. But they were all dead now.

You're pouting, Bryon, Jordan, his AI, said into his internal commlink. *Stop it, it doesn't become you. And you still have lots of friends.*

"Name three," Byron mumbled, stepping to one side, so the others didn't overhear him. He watched Professor Elmo follow Jamie towards the glass wall of doors and heard Croaker's heavy boots coming around the van. Kitty was snarling at Fritz, who in turn was cooing comforting noises at her.

Silver, Hank, and Bigfoot. Jordan sounded smug.

"His name is Frank, not Bigfoot," Bryon growled, "and none of them are friends. They're business associates or colleagues, maybe acquaintances at best."

"Talking to the voices in your head, Savage?" Croaker paused, turning enough to speak over his shoulder. "You should be careful about that. They might start talking back."

If he only knew, am I correct? Jordan's laugh that followed was hollow, mechanical, and empty, which is how Byron had programmed it. He missed his humanity and didn't want a machine being a surrogate for real interactions. *But those three, and others, could be more than acquaintances if you'd just invite them out for coffee, or hot monkey sex, or something.*

"You realize that two of the three are sexually attracted to women, and the third identifies as asexual, don't you?" Byron said, turning away from Croaker as the man continued on his way.

So, you have thought about sex, and your reply shows I was correct, Jordan said, her tone bland in his ear. *I shall deduct the appropriate amount from your accounts to cover my winnings in the bet about your humanity existing or dissipating.*

"Don't touch me," Kitty was saying to Fritz as the two shuffled past Byron, the former slapping at the latter's hands as Fritz tried to help Kitty walk. "I told you, I'm fine."

"Aw," Fritz moaned sympathetically, "like your namesake, you turn away affection, but I think you really need a kind word and a helping hand."

"You're like a fracking puppy," Kitty groaned, her voice fading as they drew away, "pawing at me and yapping to get attention. Just because you're cute doesn't mean that I…"

See? That's what friends do, whatever else Kitty said was lost in Jordan's words and the distance. *They help one another, even when one says they don't want or need help.*

Byron ignored his digital advisor and followed the others into the building, which Professor Elmo had opened and stood holding the door for the others to enter. Taking up the rear, Byron studied the interior of the University as Jordan recorded everything he looked at for later study and breakdown.

Their guide led them through long abandoned corridors, every third light in the ceiling casting a yellowed spotlight every half-dozen meters. He pointed out boring cabinets of forgotten mementos, halls of deserted classrooms without students, and bathrooms. The man seemed to have a story for each bathroom. Hauntings, genius epiphanies, or romantic rendezvous topped the list of stories of the dozen or more washrooms they passed.

Professor Elmo led them down into the depths of the building, into a warren of drab green hallways branching out into seemingly random directions. Byron had Jordan map it all, creating a partially completed 3D rendering of the complex, more of it filled in from township blueprints approved during construction.

Byron, Jordan said into his skull, *it appears you've crossed into a portion of the structure not on the official plans.*

"Mhm," Byron grunted, muttering, "not surprised. Scan for heat or radiation signatures, cycle through bandwidths."

"What was that?" Haunt said, looking back.

"Oh," Byron coughed into his fist, "I was just saying I wasn't surprised you can see tradition overtures by going through and with…um, memories…and stuff."

"You know, I'm not an idiot," Haunt sneered, "and I can't read you because of all the nanites and shit inside you, but I'm guessing you're an older model who can't talk to your AI without speaking."

"I can't talk to your mom without speaking," Byron spat, and Kitty hissed a laugh.

"What the hell is that even supposed to mean?" Jamie threw his hands up. "It makes no sense, you moron."

"It means," Professor Elmo said, "we're here. And now you each get to witness an incredible discovery that has only been witnessed by a few people a handful of times in the history of the entire planet."

The group turned to look at the professor as the man turned a doorknob and threw the door open. The smell of vinegar flooded the hallway, covering the disused and dusty scent that pervaded everything before that moment. A green pulsing light came from within, with intermittent purple flashes. The harsh crackle of electricity was mixed with the whir of machinery. Byron felt his skin rise in a wave of goosebumps.

"What the hell have you done?" Croaker grunted, stepping into the room.

Kitty squatted and spun around the doorframe, vibro-whip crackling, as Fritz darted to the other side, his hand unbuttoning his flight suit. Haunt stood on his tippytoes, leaning one way then the other, trying to see around Croaker.

"Are you fracking kidding me?" Byron heard Kitty's shrill voice echoing, then disappearing in a burst of electrical confluence.

Byron bodily moved Jamie to one side, stepping into the room.

"I wouldn't do that if I were you," he heard Jamie mutter from behind him.

"And why the hell not?" Byron's words slipped from his lips and disappeared somewhere beyond his awareness.

The room was immense, three stories tall and large enough to be a gymnasium. Byron's eyes rose to the ceiling, which was littered with skylights. Almost a third were open to the elements, lightning rods jutting above the grey, gaping openings. Walkways circled the room on four different levels, fire-escape-style stairs leading from one to the other. Each level had a jutting platform on a different wall where machinery rose to meet it. Byron assumed it was to make adjustments to the experiments done in the chamber.

Byron's gaze drifted to ground level, and he saw what the others had seen. He gasped. Without thought, his wrist rose, the mag-pulse targeting device popping open, and his other hand fell to grip the electro-stun rod on his thigh.

Hey boss, Jordan said into his comm, *ease up. Don't do anything rash without an explanation first.*

"That's Frank!" Byron blurted. "Why the hell is Frank strapped into a Frankenstein experiment bed and hooked up to all that crap?"

On the main floor beyond where Croaker, Kitty, and Fritz stood staring was a metal medical table. On that table was strapped an extremely tall and hairy man whom Byron knew pretty well. Frank had a passing resemblance to the mythical creature Bigfoot, but wasn't one of that species, though Byron was pretty sure they existed somewhere.

Arrayed around the table were whirring machines, beeping devices, and multiple immense Tesla coils connected to an immense plasma sphere. Purple arcs of electricity tickled the inside of the glass globe, and pulses of power ran along the copper columns with donut shaped toppers. In turn, they were each attached to one of the many lightning rods that rose through the ceiling to the storm outside.

"Frank," Professor Elmo began in a scholarly tone, "is experiencing a revolution in evolution. Using my own—not yet patented—inventions and altering his genetic makeup to receive the ethereal creatures from beyond the veil of worlds. Beings of pure energy—nothing but consciousness—contacted me back when the university was still housing lessons and students. It seems normal humans are not able to receive the beings who spoke to me from…"

Professor Elmo stopped lecturing suddenly as Byron shoved an electro-rod into the man's midsection.

"Cut him loose," Byron shouted, turning away from the groaning mad scientist and moving towards his restrained acquaintance. "The Midnight Progeny will have a fit when they find out what's going on here."

"Hold on," Croaker placed a restraining hand on Byron's shoulder, then ducked as the electro-rod swooshed over his head. "Listen to me, boy! We need to shut down the machine before we release him, otherwise we'll be caught in the circuit. Which may kill us, or just rewire our brains to one of the things Professor Elmo was ranting about. We're all *different* here. We may not be a perfect choice as a vessel, but I think he knew we'd be possible candidates for the same treatment."

Croaker waved a hand at five other empty tables, and a crazy laughter came from the floor behind them.

"Get them," Professor Elmo coughed, crab-crawling backwards and out of the room. "Take them and prepare them for receiving, my darlings!"

The door slammed as the group turned towards the Professor. Grinding noises joined wet slapping sounds, and the five spun back to face the room. From dark alcoves set around the space, figures lurched forward. The flickering lights of the devices caused the overhead LED lights to shudder from dim to glaringly bright.

"What the hell are those things?" Fritz yipped, moving behind Kitty, who was still crouched, but now her back was arched.

"Monsters," Haunt muttered, but loud enough for everyone to hear. "I feel them. It's like feeling rancid oil on water, or smelling sewage in a polluted city street."

The creatures shambled into the flashing light, short and slightly hunched. They wore nothing more than rubbery loin cloths that may have been neoprene or a sheet of alien flesh hanging down. Their skin was the deep green of madness, like a wet leaf at night if coated with the rainbow sheen of petrol. Webbed hands opened and closed spasmodically, and wide, short feet slapped on the discolored concrete floor.

Their heads, though, were what held everyone's attention. They were wide and flat, bulbous on the side, showing an elongated skull stretched back past their shoulders. Dark, round eyes protruded from their skulls, jerking from one person to the next. Rough, spiked tongues showed in their open mouths, a bluish glob at the tip resting on an ochre ridge of their jagged mandible.

"He's an Abby Normal, right?" Croaker asked, pointing at Frank. "An AB Normal? An adjusted biological? A mutant, right?"

"Yeah," Byron sputtered, "him and all the Midnight Progeny."

"That's what they want," Kitty hissed. "They want people who aren't the normal genetic human."

"Exactly," Croaker growled, "and here's what we're going to do…"

He was cut off as the creatures threw themselves at the group, fishhook claws popping out of their rubbery, webbed fingertips.

5. Inn Too Deep

Back at the inn, Jack stared at the screen, his hand on the pause button. He let out a ragged breath. "Well, that escalated quickly."

"Excuse me, sir," Cogsley said, drawling in his uppity way, "I think everyone was watching that. Pausing it at this moment may be considered rude."

"Durg like that play," the half-ogre chimed in from across the club, his face a mask of shifting colors in the rave lights, "and you stop it at fight part. Best part!"

"It's okay, Durg," Darome patted the big man's hand, "we'll see what's going on soon enough. Jack probably needs to pontificate upon what's going on."

"Jack needs to go potty." Durg nodded sagely. "Sometimes Durg needs to potty-fee-kate, too. It's okay, Jackie. You go poo, we gonna wait for you."

"No," Wanderly said, rolling up to the bar in a tipsy swagger, "he needs to pontificate, as in talk about something."

"Oh," Durg drew out the single syllable in understanding. "He needs to mouth potty. Okay Jack, you talk shit, and we listen."

"Yeah," Wanderly giggled, climbing up a bar stool with

his empty mug, "something like that. Good job, big guy."

Durg smiled as Wanderly held his mug towards Cogsley. "Barkeep, another round for me and my best friend. Which is me. I'll take two and maybe call you in the morning."

"Jack," Nomed said from the circular booth on the side of the Traveller's Inn, "what's on your mind?"

"I've seen these things before," Jack said absently, picking up his thoughts, "and am piecing together how they connect to the other events we've witnessed recently."

"Tilbert," Professor Elementius's harsh whisper cut through the silence, "pay attention and keep typing. This is getting good."

"Of course, sir," the young scribe nodded vigorously, his fingers clacking on his hovering keyboard. "I'm getting it all, sir."

"The first group encountered some sort of trans-dimensional spider," Jack continued. "The second group had the scarecrows who took over people's bodies. This seems to be some combination of the two. A little more direct, I think."

Nomed stood up, pushing out of the plush seating and grabbing his rock glass. He knew Jack well, had been friends with the man for…well, time was less relevant when jumping through the millennia and living in the Traveller's Inn. Something that's to be expected when you're hanging out in a time travelling, dimension hopping, semi-sentient building run by a man who had lived hundreds of years in a dozen different timelines.

"Jack," Nomed said, watching the amber liquid swirl in his glass, "you're spinning your wheels, man. I've known you for a while now, and I feel I can speak to you as an equal."

"Ha!" Wanderly's outburst made everyone turn to him. "What? I'm just wondering who is equal to who in that sentence. I mean, and don't get me wrong, I love these guys, but Nomed's ego is the size of a continent and has the force of a hurricane. Jack, on the other hand, is like the ocean tides. He's subtle, but relentless, and will change the shape of continents and guide hurricanes with the patience of centuries. So, I'm just wondering if Nomed—who has toppled Kingdoms and deterred demon lords trying to take over worlds—is saying Jack is his equal. Or is Nomed tipping his hat to Jack, saying he respects him and recognizes his-"

"Let's just say it's a bit of both, okay?" Nomed interrupted, glaring at the smaller man. "If I don't cut you off, then you'll never shut up. For a little guy, you sure can talk a lot."

"Speaking of talking a lot," Jack interrupted Nomed's interrupting, "what were you saying?"

"Right, um, ah, yeah." Nomed looked at the ceiling, trying to gather his thoughts. "What I was saying was, you need to get your head straight. You keep saying the same things over and over again. Which is fine, but we have to sit here and listen to it. Maybe it's time to ask for some help?"

"You know," Wanderly said, lowering his glass from his lips and smiling, "you do tend to try and take the weight of the world—or the weight of many worlds—on your shoulders and carry it alone. You ask us to run a mission now and then, but you never really share your burden."

Wanderly fell silent, along with the rest of the room. Besides the quiet thump of bass from the music, the only sound was Wanderly slurping from his mug.

"Make note, Tilbert," Elementius's whisper cut through the silence. "Wanderly actually stopped speaking on his own without being cut off by someone else."

"Yes, sir," Tilbert nodded, clacking, "got it."

"Okay, then," Jack spoke up, "what do you all think? And before you answer all at once," Jack held up a hand, "let's start with Nomed, since he was the one that pointed this out."

All eyes turned to the demon hybrid, who straightened up to his full height, chest muscles rippling.

"Why?" Nomed said the single word, looking around the

room with a raised eyebrow. "Why is someone targeting the Inn? You've already said they want what we have here, but why do they want it? Let's figure out their motivation. That's how I turned peasants to nobility and vice versa."

"Oh, oh, oh!" Durg raised his hand, his other hand gripping his bicep to hold his arm up. "Durg knows! Durg knows! Please, pick me. Please! Please! Please!"

"You," Nomed said in a game show host voice, pointing at the hulking man, "the handsome fellow beside the gnome, what do you think?"

"Because they want people to know how strong they are," Durg said slowly, his forehead wrinkling with the effort, "and want to make others do what they want."

"Correct!" Nomed shouted, clapping his hands. "That is a basic drive for motivation. But what do they want others to do?"

The room fell silent as everyone considered.

"Um," Tilbert said meekly, "respect them? I mean, they want the usual things, like people to do all the work so they don't have to, unlimited power and resources without working for it because they feel like they've already done enough work to deserve it. Basically, they feel entitled to everyone worshipping them and never questioning them."

"Tilbert!" Elementius admonished the younger man. "Mind your place. We're here as observers, not contributors!"

"But, sir," Tilbert pleaded, "we've observed enough to make intelligent and educated conjectures that might help these people we're…"

The young man trailed off, dropping his eyes to his brass keys, which he'd still been typing on during his brief outburst.

"Tilbert is right," Nomed said, suddenly standing over the Professor and resting a strong hand on the older man's shoulder. "I understand your reticence, Professor. But your apprentice has a valid point. That being said, it still doesn't hit the crux of the matter."

"That's a lot of very big words for a brute who muscles his ways through most problems," Elementius muttered, avoiding Nomed's eyes and shirking from his grip.

"I spend my downtime," Nomed said, returning his hand to the scholar's shoulder, "when no one can see me, plotting and thinking of ways to bring ruin to other people's plots. I'm multi-talented that way. Many have learned the error of their ways after underestimating me."

"Enough, Nomed," Jack said, and Nomed lifted his hand to pat the Professor on the head. "And thank you, Tilbert. Very insightful. Let's hear from someone else. Maybe Elementius? Do you, oh wise and learned master of the libraries and words, have wisdom to share and impart upon us stumbling and blind brutes?"

"Oh, me?" Elementius looked up at Jack, shaking his head. "No, really, I shouldn't. It really isn't my place…"

The older man trailed off, looking at his hands in his lap.

"You're the older version of Tilbert, aren't you?" Nomed asked, dropping his hand back to the man's shoulder and squeezing hard. "Why don't you go ahead and take the plunge and tell us your thoughts?"

"Nomed!" Jack's voice had a dangerous tone. "Stop touching old men and step away."

The proprietor waited while Nomed raised his hand high and away from the scholar. Shooting a dark look at Jack, he stepped away, sipping his drink.

"Thank you, Nomed," Jack smiled. "You have shown your prowess and insight with your shallow threats. Oh my god, you dumbass demon asshole, stop teasing people you know will crumble under your grip. It doesn't become someone of your stature."

The room held their collective breaths as the cambion slowly turned to Jack, his chin down and glaring from under his brows. When Jack remained smiling with his eyebrows arched, Nomed laughed and raised his glass to him.

"Asshole," Nomed said jovially, "stop calling me out in front of others. It makes me look like an idiot when I don't cut you into little, itty-bitty bits for the insult."

"Nomed," Jack sighed, "we've been through too much to bump heads instead of working together. You're here for your own reasons and agenda, and right now, that coincides with mine. Professor, I'd like to hear your thoughts, please."

Nomed watched Jack smoothly manipulate the old man, and allow himself to save face, simultaneously, and wondered what would happen if the two ever truly faced off against one another. Whatever happened, it wouldn't be pretty.

"Well," Elementius licked his lips, "I guess I would reinforce what Tilbert said," the young man looked up, surprised, "but would add that your nemesis may have personal motives for what they do. In smaller words, so the lesser among us may understand, who did you piss off that could do this?"

"Thank you, Professor," Jack inclined his head, then looked up as Wanderly wiggled and twitched on his barstool with unspoken excitement. "Okay, Wanderly, you're next."

"Oh, thank goodness!" the halfling let out an immense gust of air he'd been holding in. His next words came out in a rush. "Jack, you're a nice guy, but an idiot. They're all right, okay? This is about you, and you need to look at your past adventures and exploits to figure out who is behind all this. I was here when the Traveller's Inn was a submarine traveling through time and space before it was an entire shapeshifting building…oops, was I not supposed to say that? Anyway, you've pissed off a lot of powerful entities, in the real world and beyond, and that's who has the resources to do this sort of attack. Not someone in the real world, I mean, but someone else who can travel. I mean, can Nomed travel like you and the Inn? That would be a perfect-"

"Master Wanderly," Cogsley cut in, "you appear to be going over the same ground again. Perhaps I could offer some insight?"

"Um, sure?" Wanderly shrugged. "I forgot what my point was, anyway."

"Indeed, as did we all," Cogsley nodded his glass dome of a head, flickers of purple energy tickling the inside. "But I would offer the concept that the Inn itself may be the target of the attacks. My own source of being feels under attack by these events, and perhaps you shouldn't make it about yourself all the time?"

"Time Lords," Golem FloorSweeper mumbled in a tone that sounded depressed and resigned.

"What was that?" Nomed turned to look at the underling automaton.

"It's a Doctor Who thing, from Jack's first timeline," Golem said, shrugging their massive shoulders. "If you have warlords and peasants, gods fighting one another, then who is above each of them? The beings who can travel time, space, and realities. Like Jack. Someone gifted Jack with this Inn. But someone else wants to take it. Sounds like the enemy of your benefactor."

"I…" Jack breathed, his face confused, "have someone who is my benefactor?"

"Sure, Jack," Darome's high-pitched voice cut through the room, "we all do. And in this case, it's you. So, you must have one also. There's always a bigger fish in the sea. Can we get back to what's happening to Croaker, Kitty, and the others?"

50

6. Saint Elmo's Fire

Croaker didn't have the time or patience for this shit. He'd been facing down impossible things and improbable odds since he was a young man. That was forever ago, and it felt like he'd been an old man all his life. These kids needed direction. Whether it was Savage—he must be nearly Croaker's age, though he only looked thirty or so—who was full of bravado and bitterness, Kitty with her angst and drive, Haunt with his superior attitude, or Fritz…actually, Croaker didn't know much about Fritz, but he seemed like a good boy.

"Group up, you dolts," Croaker shouted as the group scattered. Knowing if they separated, they'd be taken down one by one. Croaker tried to give direction to the chaos. "Damn it, stop running around like morons!"

Kitty charged forward, vibro-whip snapping out to wrap around the wrist of one of the amphibian invaders. The creature made a croaking noise and spat a thick glob of viscous goo into the woman's face. Kitty's head jerked back, enveloped by the off-white substance, and she brought her free arm up to scrape at it with the barrel at the end of her wrist.

Savage beelined for Frank on the table, turning sideways

to fire the V-shaped contraption on his wrist. The air vibrated a hollow shoomp noise and a wave of vertigo rolled across Croaker and the others. Their attackers surged forward, unaffected by the dizzying pulse attack.

Haunt pressed backwards against the door, his hand jiggling the knob, which didn't turn. Spinning around, he tried to open it with both hands when he went down under a tackle of two of the monsters.

Fritz ran for a metal stairway leading up to the next level and a half-dozen creatures broke away to give chase to the small man.

Croaker was about to shout again when three of the attackers came towards him. Squaring off, Croaker patted the various pockets in his trench coat and pants before reaching into the satchel hanging over his shoulder. His mind ran in circles. Usually, he had gadgets prepared for what was coming, but this was a complete surprise and he hadn't had time to cobble anything together.

Pulling a handful of jerky from his bag, Croaker threw them at the fish-men. The strips and clumps of dried meat pelted the creatures, and one wiped its thick tongue across its eye, catching a piece of jerky and dragging it into its mouth.

Croaker felt a wash of warm liquid flow across his boots, and looking down he saw that the floor was covered with a thin layer of briny water.

"This whole place is a huge electrical conductor," he muttered, then looked around again.

The creature who Kitty faced had wrapped her vibro-whip around its wrist and Croaker could see blue sparks bouncing off its rubbery skin. Kitty couldn't retract the whip, or use the hand it was attached to, and had sunk to her knees, trying to breathe through the goop mask covering most of her face. One wild eye rolled in her head and stopped on Croaker, a pleading look crossing her expression.

"Okay, one thing at a time," Croaker muttered, then

raised his voice. "Fritz, you're our lookout. Call out where they are. Savage, don't touch that machine…"

Turning to look at the bounty hunter, he saw the big man gripping Frank's restraints, the flow of electricity locking Savage's body into a bowed rictus, the man rising on his tippytoes. Croaker heard Haunt scream, a loud, piercing sound, as the creatures clawed at him and left thin, bloody lines with their razor claws.

Kitty was closest, so Croaker decided to help her first. Right after he dealt with the three coming at him. He pulled a short, thick club—the kind used by fishermen to pummel their catch—from inside his coat, and a handful of sharpened children's jacks from his satchel. Tossing the makeshift caltrops across the floor, he swung the cudgel at the leading fish-thing.

The lead attacker flapped across the small, sharpened metal bits and let out a gurgled growl, teetering to one side and breaking off its attack. A second one came at Croaker through the cleared path, and the old man completed his swing, catching the beast in a bulging eye. The black orb burst with a pop and the creature stumbled to the side.

The third monster slowed, its eyes swiveling in their sockets to its companions. It drew in a breath as it refocused on Croaker, and the man could hear it gathering mucus. The slow, throaty noise of a loogie being formed made Croaker charge forward—his thick-soled boots protecting him from the caltrops—and slammed the end of his club into the creature's throat right as it opened its mouth to spit.

The monster choked, trying to spit and swallow at the same time.

While the creature was distracted, Croaker dropped the club, so it swung on its strap from his wrist and darted to Kitty's side. He pulled a flask from the breast pocket of his coat, and a six-shooter from the holster on his hip. He pressed the gun to the head of the creature attacking Kitty and pulled the trigger at point blank range.

The monster jerked away from the woman, half of its

head missing. She stared at him, pale and her single uncovered eye wide, and blinked in confusion at the container in his hand.

"Stay still, girl," he grumbled, splashing the bourbon across her face. The phlegm coating bubbled and thinned, and Croaker dragged the flat edge of the flask down the woman's face, pulling the suffocating sputum away from her nose and mouth.

She reached up with her hand—now freed of restraint and the inactive vibro-whip trailing in the water—and pulled more of the goo away.

"No electricity," Croaker said, jabbing her in the shoulder with a stubby finger as she gasped for breath. He raised the flask and took a deep drink, then stood and leveled his pistol towards the door.

"No time for clean shots," Croaker growled, and three more shots rang out.

The creatures on Haunt jerked and spun towards Croaker. Aiming, he fired again and the monster's head exploded. He shifted the gun a finger-width to the side, and another went down in a spray of gore. The third burst through the rain of brain matter, launching itself directly at Croaker, fingers splayed and claws glinting in the weird, flickering light. The gun clicked again but didn't fire.

A flare of bright white light cut through the air from over Croaker's shoulder, causing him to close his eyes and jerk his head to the side to avoid being blinded. A heavy weight hit Croaker and he fell backwards under the beast. As he struggled to throw the monster off, he realized it wasn't fighting back. It was dead weight, and he rolled it off with ease.

Blinking, Croaker looked up to see Kitty's silhouette standing over him in a halo of double negative imagery, and green and purple light pulsing behind her.

"Need a hand, old man?" she coughed, her voice thick.

"Yeah," Croaker took her offered hand, and she pulled him to his feet. "Check on Savage, but don't touch him if he's still playing pet lightning rod."

Kitty nodded and slinked away.

Croaker dug a quick-load from his belt, flicked his firearm open and dumped the shells, and slammed the new rounds home. Flicking it closed, he turned to survey the room.

It had been less than a minute since the door closed, and the room was only slightly less chaotic than thirty seconds ago. Haunt was pushing to his feet, his face ashen as he ran his hands along his shredded outfit. They came away red with his blood and dark gobs of fish-men parts fell to the floor. Savage gripped the table restraints, but had both feet on the floor. He was moving as though in slow motion.

Kitty stepped up beside him, leaning to look around him, and raised her arm cannon. Another silent burst of light came from her built-in weapon and a sparking explosion showered down as the machinery over Frank shuddered. The lights around the table dimmed and faded as the connection was severed. Savage burst into superhuman speed, tearing the leather cuffs from the bolts on the gurney. The bounty hunter scooped up his friend and looked back at Croaker. A severed arm splattered against his head, followed by a foot and half a head.

Looking up, Croaker saw a rain of alien body parts tumbling down from the third level. Animalistic growls and short barking noises echoed with a rumble of thunder.

"What the hell is going on up there?" Jamie said from over Croaker's shoulder.

"No idea," Croaker shrugged, returning his attention to the creatures on the main floor. "But I think Fritz has it handled. We need to take these guys out."

Kitty laughed, pointing. "Looks like we've already got them on the run."

The fish-men were beating a retreat back to the alcoves where they'd come from, and Croaker smiled. His amusement and relief were short-lived as the hidden cubbies lit up with the purplish arcs of electricity that had surrounded Frank moments before. A dozen other gurneys showed in the nooks, each with a person strapped to it, as the fish-men flipped huge levers within, then dropped down bolt holes in the floor.

The people on the tables lit up like Christmas lights. Strobing greens and purples bled through the skin, shining from inside the restrained victims. They opened their mouths to scream, their eyes flared wide, but only more light came out.

"No!" Savage said. "They're all Midnight Progeny!"

Lightning flashed overhead and was immediately followed by a deafening clap of thunder. The building shook as nature's raw power surged downward along the wires and apparatus, turning the room as bright as day. Croaker shielded his eyes, and when he looked back up, spots danced in his vision. The machinery pulsed, pushing waves of green energy up and out of the building. The clouds washed with the color, changing and shifting until they glowed with that same otherworldly light from within.

A deep thrum filled the room, a rhythmic and ominous sounding whine rising from the machinery. The sound increased in intensity, and Croaker looked around.

"Okay folks," Croaker raised his voice to be heard, "we need to get out of here, now!"

"Yah," Fritz said from Croaker's elbow, causing the man to do a double take. "I tink that this is more dangerous than we can handle."

The small man was naked except for a lime green pair of speedos. His tattered flight suit hung from one hand, and he was covered with chunks of fish-men and dripped dark ichor from his hirsute limbs and chest.

"Right," Croaker nodded, then shook his head. "Savage, give your friend to Kitty. She can carry him. You get that door open. Just don't use anything that uses electricity."

Savage nodded and passed Frank to the street samurai, being gentle with the unconscious man. Kitty took the prisoner, who was almost twice her size, as Savage stomped towards the door. With a low growl, the bounty hunter drew back his arm. Making a fist, he punched downward at the knob with one hand, while simultaneously punching the middle hinge with his other fist and kicking at the lower hinge. The door exploded outwards, the third hinge tearing free and skittering down the hall outside.

The group rushed into the hall, exiting in the direction they'd come. Savage turned and took Frank back from Kitty, tossing him over his shoulder in a fireman's carry.

"Anyone recall the way?" Croaker asked.

"Oh, yah," Fritz chimed, looking happy to help. "We just need to follow my nose!"

The small man threw his shredded flight suit over his shoulder and ran down the hall. That's when things began exploding.

7. Abby Normal

The cinder block walls cracked and chunks of mortar tumbled to the floor around the fleeing group. Fritz led the way, taking turns at full speed, his toenails clattering on the concrete floor as he skidded around the corners. Kitty was right behind him, followed by Savage carrying Frank, Jamie, and Croaker lagged behind, puffing in an effort to keep up.

Kitty wanted to shove the runt out of the way, but knew she'd get lost. Besides, he seemed to know where he was going. A hunk of wall exploded, the steel box holding the fire extinguisher shooting across the hall directly in front of Kitty. It slammed into the far wall and engaged, spinning in a circle as it spewed a chemical cloud.

They kept running.

Looking around, Kitty wondered what the strategy was once they got out of the building. Was the plan ruined? Was the mission over? She looked around for Croaker, wanting to ask him what they'd do next. He wasn't there. He was the only one she trusted or cared about, and she'd be damned if she was leaving without him. Croaker would tell her she should care about others, tell her that not caring or trusting would eat her up inside. But she didn't care. Just trusting him was enough for her.

They reached a set of stairs and Fritz bounded up them, using his hands to assist in his climb. Kitty waved Savage and his burden past her, then grabbed Jamie's arm, stopping him.

"Let go," Jamie spat through gritted teeth and pulled out of her grip. "We need to get out of here."

She grabbed him again.

"Where's Croaker?" Kitty hissed.

"Who cares?" Jamie shot back. "If he can't keep up, that's not my fault."

The man jerked away again and she let him go, looking back the way they'd come. The air was thick with dust and ruptured pipes misting the hall with a fine spray of water.

Kitty headed back into the tunnel. She'd only taken a few steps when she saw death itself approaching. The creature had bug-like eyes and a snout ending in two rounded protrusions. A cloak flared out from it, and Kitty's skin crawled as the figure was lit by the flicking emergency lights, shifting from a dark shadow to an ominous shade of red.

"Get the hell out of here," Kitty heard Croaker shout, startling her. The figure flapped both arms at her, as if waving her away. "Damn it, girl. You look like you've seen the Devil himself behind me."

"Oh, frak!" Kitty gasped. "It's you, Croaker!"

"Yeah, I'm just guarding our flank," Croaker said, the terrifying form coalescing into the slightly hunched shape of her friend. "I wouldn't leave you. I just move a bit slower. Now, go on. Catch up with the others. I'll be along shortly. I just don't move as quick as you young people."

"We'll go together," Kitty said, ushering the older man past her and up the stairs. "Besides, I want to know what the plan is."

"The plan is to get the hell out of Dodge," Croaker said, moving up the stairs and leaning heavily on the railing.

"No shit, Sherlock," Kitty grinned. "But after that? Once we're out, what are we gonna do?"

"One thing at a time, Kitty," Croaker said, the words

coming haltingly as he moved past the landing and began the climb to the ground floor.

She stopped asking questions, letting Croaker save his breath for the climb. She could hear him gasping and hoped it was the gas mask he wore causing it. The building rumbled again, and Kitty wasn't sure if it was another collapse or the thunderstorm outside.

They left the stairwell and came into the hall lined with trophy cases and memorabilia of the school's forgotten conquests. The orangey Berber carpet squished with every step, and small waterfalls poured from the ceiling, sparking where it touched torn wiring. They weaved through the hall, dodging obstacles and picking up the pace slightly. Pale light showed ahead.

"We're almost at the main entrance, Croaker," Kitty said, trying to encourage her friend.

"Don't baby me," Croaker grumped. "I'm old, not blind or stupid. I can see we're almost there."

They came to the main foyer and wind grabbed at Croaker's trench coat. Glass littered the wide entryway, sheets of rain washing past the shattered windows and doors. Only four of the six columns remained. The other two were broken, the tops clinging precariously to the ceiling, the bottoms looking like the sundered teeth of a long dead dragon. The faded red carpet running down the center looked like a tongue, completing the imagery for Kitty.

They crunched across the shards and Croaker pulled his coat closed, like the cloak of an ancient traveler. He paused, lifted his fedora, pulled the gasmask off and, coughing, crammed it into his satchel. He replaced the hat on his head as they stepped from the building.

The others stood waiting under the carport, which gave next to no protection from the storm's rage. They looked at Kitty, then at Croaker, then back at Kitty, each with a concerned look. Except for the Haunt, who was picking at his tattered expensive clothes, disgusted.

"He's fine," Kitty said, patting Croaker's shoulder.

"Don't humor me, or them, girl," Croaker said, pulling away. "But I'm fine. She's right about that. Now we need to get somewhere dry, and preferably somewhere we can eat and clean up. Fritz, we need transportation. And not a TuberLyt. I don't want everyone on the interwebs seeing a vid of us looking like drowned rats who just got hit with a smoke bomb.

"Yah, I'm on it, boss." Fritz nodded vigorously and dug in a pocket of his flight suit, which he now wore. The small man stepped away, murmuring into his cardphone.

"I don't think we can just take Frank to a Twaffle House," Savage said, looking down at his hairy, unconscious friend propped against his legs. "We should contact the Midnight Progeny. They need to know what happened."

"Yeah, we will," Croaker nodded. "But we want to do that on our terms. Which, if that means a Twaffle House, it's not like anyone would question us looking like this. I'm sure they see worse almost every Saturday night when bars let out."

"He's not wrong," Haunt said, looking up. "I've done a lot of things in Twaffle Houses, and this wouldn't be the worst."

"Okay, dere is dah good news and dah bad news," Fritz said, returning to the group. He continued before anybody could voice their preference of which he conveyed first. "Dah bad news is dat the police are coming this way, and each of you people have been fingered, and fingered hard, by a mystery person. It seems dat you people each have been doing human experiments on people who are not willing."

"You keep saying you people, like you're not being targeted by the authorities," Savage said, and Kitty glared at him.

"Yah, dat is correct." Fritz nodded vigorously. "It seems dat only you people were caught on the cameras. Not a single one saw me. It appears my tiny, wee man height kept me behind all of you people whenever there were dah cameras."

"Convenient," Haunt muttered. "I smell a setup."

"You smell all right," Fritz agreed, wrinkling his nose. "You smell like dah wet fishes."

"Aren't all fish wet?" Kitty asked.

"I meant dat Haunt smells dah fishiest," Fritz explained, "because a camera caught him with a demon on a leash."

"A what?" Croaker coughed.

"Yah," Fritz nodded vigorously again, "if it is dah faking, den it is very, very, very, very good. If it is not dah faking, then I want everyone to know right now that Haunt is my new best friend."

"And what's the good news?" Savage growled.

"Oh, dat?" Fritz grinned a lopsided smile. "I made a call to a friend and we have a hover-van with full riot gear showing up. My friend got us dah startup and login codes."

"Well," Croaker said, "that is good news. When does it show up?"

"With the rest of the policemen," Fritz nodded. "It's dere SWAT unit, and once they all get here and go inside, we can just jump in and zoom away."

"Hold on," Kitty stepped in front of Fritz, blocking the others from reaching him first. "So, the cops are on the way, with SWAT and riot gear. Once they're here, we steal their best armed and armored vehicle from their command circle in an empty parking lot with no cover. Is that the plan?"

"All while carrying an unconscious over two-meter-tall man," Savage added. "And my AI is out of commission, so she can't help talk to the SWAT van's computer."

"Dat's right!" Fritz clapped his hands and did a little jump. "It's very exciting. I can't wait to see how you people do this!"

"Me, too!" Kitty squealed, also clapping and giving a little hop. "Do we want to do it with a big explosion, or with a distraction? Oh, I know, we can use a small German guy on fire to be the distraction!"

"Wait, no," Fritz shook his head, "I don't think I can get you one of those very quickly, and I'm not volunteering for that, either."

"Group vote would overrule the volunteering part," Haunt said, leaning around Kitty to glare at Fritz.

"I can work with this," Croaker said.

"You can?" Kitty turned to her mentor. "Savage is out of commission. Fritz is useless, and you are still gasping to breathe. That leaves me as muscle and firepower—and I only have one shot remaining in my arm cannon. Oh, and Haunt and his pet demon."

"Do you really have a demon?" Croaker asked, turning to Haunt. "Or is that just more bullshit?"

"Well, she's not really a demon per se," Haunt shrugged, looking behind him. "She's more of a ball of emotion and residue that showed up and began following me."

"Can this thing do anything?" Croaker asked.

"She tends to only up the ante on other people's emotions," Haunt explained. "Makes whatever they're feeling more intense."

"Great," Croaker nodded. "We'll use that. Get her locked and loaded and set her loose on the authorities remaining in the parking lot once the others enter the building. Oh, and speaking of which…"

Croaker paused, raising a finger to forestall anyone from talking, then pointed into the night. The sound of distant sirens drew everyone's attention.

"Less than three minutes, I'd guess by the sound." Croaker turned in a slow circle. "We'll need cover, and the closer to the parking lot, the better."

The old man dropped his satchel and gingerly knelt beside it. He began digging through it, pulling out odd pieces, and either returning them to his bag or snapping them together.

"Shouldn't we hide?" Haunt asked.

"Sh," Kitty held up a hand to the man, her eyes still on Croaker and a huge grin on her face. "This is what he does. He cobbles crazy shit together."

"Get to the bushes," Croaker flapped his hand towards

three leaf-bare shrubs to one side of the entrance, "I'll be done in about two minutes."

"Two minutes?" Savage said, looking towards the approaching sirens. "They'll be here in about that much time. And those bushes might hide one of us, two if one of them is Fritz. There are no leaves, and they're only waist height."

"Then you should hurry," Croaker said. "Don't make me wait on you."

Savage picked up Frank and carried him to the sparse cover, Kitty, Fritz, and Haunt following. The four crouched behind the barren shrubbery, Frank laid on the ground in front of them.

Blue lights swam across the buildings closest to the University as Croaker rose and limped towards the group, a metal box the size of a three-ring binder in his hands.

"Okay everyone," Croaker said, his gnarled finger on a toggle switch, "stay as still as you can, and no one sneeze."

Croaker flipped the switch, set the box on the desiccated mulch in front of the bushes, and shuffled behind them to stand beside the others.

Kitty blinked at a sheet of haze in front of the bushes. It was very similar to the one caused by the gray drizzle but going from the ground up. Barely visible in the rain, she wasn't sure how it was going to help them. Savage and Haunt crouched, and Kitty hunched down a little. Only Croaker and Fritz stood at their full height, which, for Fritz, was about the same as the others who had crouched and hunched.

A dozen vehicles spun into the parking lot, silencing their sirens and light and zooming up to the covered carport outside of the main entrance.

"Oh, fuck," Savage growled, "it's the T.A.L.O.N. Agency. Fritz, you little bastard, you didn't say it would be them!"

"Who?" Kitty whispered.

"Shush," Croaker shushed, and pointed at the figures

pouring out of the vehicles. "Just stay quiet, very still, and watch."

8. Mad Hunt

Fritz looked back and forth between the vehicles crowding the area outside the carport and directly in front of the entryway. Uniformed figures leapt from three box trucks, each painted dark with tinted windows. Men and women in suits stepped from the various other vehicles. Umbrellas came up, and a few stepped gingerly to avoid dipping expensive shoes into puddles.

An older man barked orders. He was broad-shouldered and gray at the temples, but looked like he wrestled bears for fun. One van had people in white hazmat suits rolling out a canopy with walls and a floor to create a clean-room environment, another erected a pop up with walls, then set up tables with sophisticated equipment. The third hovered above the asphalt, and a line of armed and armored men and women dropped out of it and lined up under the carport.

"That one's ours," Fritz whispered, pointing at the last vehicle. Kitty wrapped a hand around his face and covered his mouth.

In less than five minutes, the group set up the science van. The communications and surveillance team were at computers clacking away, and the soldiers were heading into the building in a leapfrog formation.

Croaker knelt, shifting the haze device to an angle that kept them hidden from those entering the building, in case they looked back. Fritz slipped out the other side and darted to the front of a car, barely needing to duck to stay out of sight.

"What's he doing?" Fritz heard Haunt ask. "He's going to get us all killed. Or worse, caught by the T.A.L.O.N. Agency!"

"Shush," came Kitty's response from behind him, "or you'll do it for him!"

The older man who'd been giving orders glanced towards the bushes and everyone went quiet. The burly man took a few steps toward the concealed bunch, staring at the apparently empty area.

"Sir," a young woman said to the man's back, "the team is entering the stairwell. Cams are up, but we're experiencing some weird interference."

"What sort of weird interference?" the man asked, turning back towards the comms tent. "Have any of our brain trust picked up on anything that would cause it?"

He strode back to the comms tent, looking over the woman's shoulder at a glowing screen.

"They are saying the entire campus is radiating at least three different wavelengths that could cause it," the woman replied, pointing at a beeping device beside the screen. "Plus, the storm is throwing out a lot of electrical interference. Any of them could be the cause."

"Relay to the team to drop boosters every ten meters," the commander grunted. "Send the message through their headsets and type it to their HUDs, as well."

"Of course, sir," she replied, tapping at the table where the light-keyboard was projected, "already on it."

"Good job," the officer nodded, "we don't want the Midnight Progeny getting away again, or anything else in this mess."

Fritz, seeing the man had his back to the group, waved for the others to follow him. Kitty darted forward, making it to where Fritz was waiting. Croaker, holding Frank's feet, came next, Savage following and carrying the unconscious man under the armpits. Only Haunt remained, who hesitated, then froze, looking at the officer in charge.

Looking back to the comms tent, Fritz saw the man in charge studying the bushes again. The commander turned away to walk around the table, and Fritz frantically waved for Haunt to run to them. Haunt bent double and ran to the group, as Fritz duck-walked around the side of the car, the others following.

The commander came around the table and walked through the sheets of rain towards the group's original hiding place. Peeking over the hood of the car they hid behind, Fritz could see the holographic blind Croakers had cobbled together wavering, and dead branches sticking through it where Croaker had adjusted it earlier. The rest of the branches behind the blind looked like healthy holly bushes, deep green with bright red berries.

Fritz eyed the distance to their goal: the SWAT van. It hung in the air—an arm's length above the ground—between the science and the comms vans. Between there and where Fritz crouched were three more cars, parked in a staggered triangle pattern. They had to move past the cars without attracting attention, and the way the agents had parked should allow that easily if they stayed on the outside of the triangle.

Fritz smiled and started off, leading the way for the others. They duck-walked to the next vehicle, staying below its windows. Croaker groaned, and Fritz looked back to see the older man rubbing at his knees. Croaker saw him looking, scowled, and waved for him to continue. Fritz scampered to the next car, and the others followed.

Only one more to go, Fritz thought. *This is going easier than I thought it would.*

"What the hell?" Fritz heard the commander bark and poked his head up to see what the man was yelling about.

The commander was waving his hand through the blur

of greenery, then pushed his head through the haze of the digital blind. The man bent over, digging in the mulch for something, and came up with a box the size of a notebook.

"Aw, shit," Croaker moaned, also looking through the windows at the commanding officer, "the jig is up."

"And gone," Haunt said, standing and bolting for their final destination.

"No, wait!" Croaker hissed, then sighed. "Too late. We're doing this the down-and-dirty way."

"Hold Frank," Savage said, shoving the big man into Kitty's care. "Get him to the van. I'll be the distraction." Without waiting to see if anyone responded, the bounty hunter stood, flipped up his wrist targeting device and let loose with a pulse towards the comms booth. He flipped his wrist in the other direction and small needles flew towards the command center with audible puffs.

Fritz had researched each person Jack told him would be on the team, and Fritz was good at what he does. So, he knew the mag-pulse would cause dizziness and disorientation to people, but he'd never seen it in action and was curious. He popped up to his full height, eyes wide, and mouth open in excitement, his tongue sticking out a little bit.

"Haunt," Croaker shouted, standing with Frank's legs in his hands and running forward, "release your girl. Set the demon on them!"

Kitty jogged along behind Croaker, stumbling under the awkward burden and trying to keep up.

"I'll do it once I'm inside and safe!" Haunt yelled over his shoulder, reaching for the van's door handle.

"No," Fritz yelped, looking towards the man, "you don't want to do that!"

Fritz bolted towards Haunt, hoping to reach him before…too late. Haunt grabbed the handle and tugged on it. The van's automated defenses kicked in, delivering a debilitating shock to the would-be intruder. Haunt did a little jig, gripping the handle, then let go and accordioned to the wet asphalt as Fritz reached him.

"Haunt," Fritz said, lifting the man's head to rest in his lap, "are you okay?"

"She's…" Haunt breathed, "loose."

Thunder boomed. It wasn't loud, but it felt close and Fritz's stiff hair moved in a breeze that made him think of a car passing in the road when he was standing on the curb. A wash of emotions came over Fritz as the gust subsided. The urge to run clashed with a throaty growl from deep inside the man.

"Oh, no, no, no," Fritz chanted, "we can't be having that. I must stay in control. Like my mother used to always say, 'Don't be a little bitch and let someone tell you when you get hot or not, wee little tater tot.' I miss my momma."

Fritz swallowed down his reactions and stood to reach for the keypad underneath the door handle. He couldn't reach. Looking around, his eyes landed on Haunt.

"Come on, big guy," Fritz said, squatting beside the dazed man, "give me a leg up, yah?"

Fritz rolled Haunt toward the van and over to his stomach. Standing, Fritz stepped up on Haunt's shoulder and rose on his tippytoes to punch in the control code.

Shouts and screams from the makeshift compound made Fritz turn and look as the door unlocked. The people within the command tent were reeling and stumbling around in a daze. The scientists in hazmat suits were clamoring to get out of their clean-room environment, odd gadgets and gizmos in their hands. They chased one another or the folks in the suits, shouting.

"Are they," Croaker panted as he came alongside the van, still carrying Frank, "really yelling for those other people to stop so they can science them?"

"That guy is screaming that he 'just wants to do science', but, yeah, basically," Kitty pointed with her chin, then gave a nudge with Frank's top half. "Let's get him into the van before they get their shit together and come for us."

"Yah," Fritz nodded, not taking his eyes off the chaos,

"the back is open."

Fritz pondered his own urges moments ago. And that was just in the passing of whatever Haunt had let off its leash. The fight-or-flight instinct had been so strong, he'd almost let go and either ran away or tore into anyone nearby. Now, here were all these other people, having uncontrolled emotional responses under the tender ministrations of some sort of supernatural emotional demon.

The people in the suits seemed to be the ones affected the most. Three stood in place, wailing like lost children, one with a spreading wet spot in his pants. Another was stripping down, ripping off her suit jacket, then her blouse, which got caught on her shoulder holster. She went into a tantrum, screaming and stomping that nothing was fair. That was when two of the white-suited science people pounced on her and scienced the hell out of her. Aliens and their anal probes have nothing on what humans on an emotional roller coaster can do to someone.

"Come on, short stuff," Savage growled, sidling up beside Fritz, "let's get in the van and get out of here. I call shotgun. Literally, because if there's a shotgun strapped in there, I'm taking it."

"Yah, right," Fritz nodded, and reached up to open the door, "we should be going now."

"Get the hell off of me," Haunt muttered below Fritz, raising his head as he came back to his senses.

"Oh, tank ya," Fritz said and stepped on the top of the man's head to boost himself into the cab of the hover-van. "Oh, and you might want to get in soon, because we are leaving now, okay?"

Fritz settled into the driver's seat, closed the door, and keyed in the access code, then switched everything to hand controls. Looking into the rearview panels, he saw Croaker helping Haunt into the back, and the empty parking lot behind the van. Savage slammed the passenger door, dropping into his seat.

"Okay, where to?" Fritz asked, looking at Savage.

The bounty hunter sighed and flicked at his wrist comm where most people kept their cardphones.

"Here," he said, "that's the coordinates to a meeting place for the Midnight Progeny. I'll give them a heads-up that we're on our way."

"Are they friends?" Fritz asked.

"No," Savage sighed again, "but they have no love for the Empire."

9. Bad Haunt

Jamie held his head in his hands as Fritz turned the van into the underground garage. It'd been a rough day. First, he had to spend time with the uncultured brute of a bounty hunter. Savage was an appropriate name; Byron was undeserved when compared to the class of the poet. Then, he was forced to ride in a minivan with a mad scientist as the chauffer. After that, sentient fish sticks attacked him and messed up his favorite suit, which cost a bundle. And lastly, he'd been soaked by rain, tasered by a van of the agency hunting him, and walked on by the runt of the litter. The only good thing was he'd managed to lose the bundle of emotional damage that had been following him around for more than a year.

He didn't care about any of these people and was only part of the team because of the money. Saving the world from boogie men and Ghostbusters big-screen enemies was optional. He'd researched each and every one of his 'companions', using mundane means and his supernatural network of spirits. He knew Croaker came from somewhere else. And not Illinois or the French Rivera. Savage was a top-notch private eye with a screw loose. But the man also had underground ties to a band of mutants called the

Midnight Progeny. They were like that old movie, Nightbreed, and Jamie had done some digging. He knew who the local cell was and had prepared to deal with them if needed. Mister Spitz was the one, oddly enough, that Jamie respected the most. That little bastard knew his shit and could get things done. Kitty, on the other hand, was a literal loose cannon that could go off about anything.

"We're here!" Fritz said in a singsong voice, then dropped to a more serious tone. "And judging by their looks and all the guns pointing at me, I don't think they are happy to see us."

"Frank," Savage said, his voice his usual angry moan, "get up here and tell your people we're the good guys and saved you."

"Um, yeah, sure," the smelly behemoth said from the floor between the benches running the length rear of the van. "On my way."

"Okay, this is ridiculous," Jamie said. "I'm tired of dicking around. It's time for the Haunt to take charge."

"Sit down, Haunt," Croaker said, grabbing Jamie's shredded sleeve, "let them take care of this the right way, instead of you just pissing everyone off. Again."

Jamie jerked his arm away, bent, and flung open the back doors. He dropped to the ground, straightened his tattered suit, and decided to take a different route. These weren't people of means. These were less than common people. These creatures, things if you will, were closer to animals living in the sewers than anybody who paid overpriced rent and struggled from paycheck to paycheck from some mega-corp. He knew how to handle them.

Pausing, he peeled off his jacket—that probably cost more than the poor wage-slaves earned in a month—and dropped it to the ground. He rolled up the stained sleeves of his satin shirt, popped his neck once in each direction, then tucked his thumbs into his waistband and turned to walk to the front of the van.

Jamie knew the streets. He'd been raised on the streets,

and he fracking hated them. When he'd first discovered his abilities, he'd decided to use them in a way that he'd never want for money again. He manipulated emotions to trigger sadness and fear, creating the environment in which people could feel their lost loved ones.

His empathy—like telepathy, but for feelings—let him understand their pain and fears. He used his minor talent for telekinesis to make a specific, special objects move at the perfect, right moment, so the mark believed exactly what he wanted them to believe. And they paid him. They'd pay him to put the spirit of their grandfather to rest. Or to chase off their angry mother, so she'd never drunkenly beat them again, even as a ghost. He'd been the best con in town at this game, and he knew his stuff.

He came around the van, taking in the three freaks standing in front of him. One was a middle-aged man with a goatee and curled horns. Markus, Jamie knew that was the man's name. Jackson was the emaciated husk beside him, like a mummy come to life. Jackson had taken the name from the character in Stargate, the archaeologist and astrophysicist. Jackson was over a thousand years old and had been locked in a tomb for over three thousand years. He could create diseases that made the bubonic plague look like a lullaby. Then there was Lulu, the pale, plain-Jane midwestern, middle-aged mom who could cause you to fall in love with her with the exchange of bodily fluids, as long as they touched a mucous membrane of her target. Her favorite was to spit in a person's mouth while they were talking. She got off on control.

"Lulu," Jamie said, raising his hands and catching the globule of phlegm that hurtled towards him, "you look as radiant as ever. I can feel the animal magnetism between us. Can you feel it?"

Jamie leaned into her emotions, tickling her urge to be dominated. That was one she suppressed, instead pushing her domination urge. Apparently, her father had been a real treat. Jamie tripped every wire he found in her psyche, which made him the opposite, yet equal, to her father. In her head, he was just like her father, but the good version.

He watched her expression melt from a stern and determined matron to a doe-eyed, lovesick schoolgirl.

"Jackson," Jamie took a moment to bow, his arms crossed over his heart, "the winds of the plains turn to dry fire and consume. But they cannot consume what is already reaped."

The words came to Jamie's head. It was some sort of ancient greeting, warped by Jackson's personal mythology and trauma. The ancient man had never put it into words, but that didn't bother Jamie. He did it for Jackson, who now stared at Jamie like he was some sort of legendary hero returned in a new form. Jamie nodded and pushed on that feeling, and Jackson fell into line.

"Markus," Jamie said, turning to the leader and dropping his gentle net of perception across the man, and it hit a stone. It was like tossing a fishing line with bait into a dry and cracked riverbed. "Okay, Markus…you're the toughest, strongest, and least susceptible to bullshit man I've ever encountered. Built Ram tough, eh?"

The man smiled at Jamie.

Jamie hit a wall with Markus, but that was only with his talents. Jamie had been a conman and a swindler long before he had developed—or been infected with, whatever— abilities that allowed him to manipulate others. Toying with people's emotions was something that came naturally to him. And he'd never failed. Except once, and she'd broken his heart. Jamie had vowed he'd never be that weak again.

"…and then we will eat, yes?" Markus was asking him something, his accent thick and rich.

"I'm sorry." Jamie shook his head and looked down, feigning embarrassment. "Your voice, your accent…it's mesmerizing. Where are you from? I must know. Wait, no. Please, repeat what you said, and let's get your friend Frank inside where it's safe."

Jamie paused, looking at Markus with a smile, hoping

he'd said the right thing.

"I said to bring Frank inside, the same as you said." Markus regarded Jamie, who had to wonder if he'd gone too far. "Byron, it's good to see you. Please, bring Frank and let us relax and be done."

Jamie turned in time to be pushed aside by Savage carrying Frank, the others trailing close behind. Lulu and Jackson closed the circle leaving Jamie to follow the group.

They entered the garage's stairwell and ducked behind the lowest set of steps. Markus opened a short, square maintenance door under the stairs, and ducked inside. He reached out to take Frank from Savage, and the bounty hunter surrendered the unconscious man's top half, squatting and duck walking through the doorway, still holding the man's legs.

Fritz popped in after, barely ducking, followed by the others. Croaker bent double to push through the door and groaned a little, and left Jamie outside by himself. Lulu's hand swept out of the hole, reaching for Jamie, who took her hand and allowed himself to be guided in.

After moving along a dark, downward-sloped concrete passage for about thirty paces, they came into a well-lit bunker. Lulu still held Jamie's hand and pulled him tight against her. Rising on her tippytoes, she pressed her lips to his, surprising him as her tongue slipped into his mouth.

Jamie's head swam, and he felt himself melt against her, his hand sliding to the back of her neck as he bent his neck to return the kiss. He pressed his hips against hers and felt their bodies reacting to each other.

"Oh, gawd, ew!" Kitty said, tugging on Jamie's arm, pulling the two apart. "Stop that. You just met her. What's wrong with you?"

"Now," Lulu said, glancing down demurely, her eyes settling on the front of Jamie's trousers, and blushing, "we're both smitten. Seems only fair, right? One kiss, and the gentle blush and blossom of love?"

"One kiss?" Croaker scoffed. "You two were going at it

for almost five minutes. Thought you were about to peel off your clothes and climb on top of Frank to get nasty."

Jamie looked around and saw Frank laid out on the couch behind him. He was sitting on the arm of the couch and Lulu had climbed onto his lap, straddling him. The dull throbbing in his midsection suggested Croaker might not be far off from the truth. Even now, Jamie had the urge to pull Lulu back to him and begin undressing her and himself. He looked around for a more private place to take her, and noticed everyone watching him, bemused smiles on their faces.

"As I had been saying," Markus said, as if he'd been interrupted, "we'll keep the van. We need it for the cause more than you guys do. But we've got another vehicle that should be large enough to fit all of you when you leave."

"We appreciate it," Savage said, reaching out and shaking Markus's hand. "We need to figure where out the Professor went."

"This place," Jamie said, lifting his chin and closing his eyes, "smells like spirits. I can hear the muted mumble of them everywhere. But they're upset. Riled up by something."

"Could be your huge presence," Lulu said, giving his crotch a squeeze. Jamie hadn't realized she was still pressed to him, her back against his chest, and she was making small swirling motions with her butt, rubbing against his goods.

"Uh," Jamie moaned, then pushed her away from him. He stood, and she leaned back again. "No, I need to think Lulu. Just for a minute." He pushed her forward again, one hand on her neck, the other on her waist, and she bent at the hips.

"Can we get a bucket of ice water or separate these two?" Croaker asked.

"It'd be amusing if it wasn't so awkward," Kitty said. "I mean, they both keep moaning every time they move."

Jamie looked down and Savage's muscular arm blocked his view of Lulu's curvy bottom. The woman stepped away, guided by Markus and Jackson, the bounty hunter stopping Jamie from following again.

"What are you feeling, Haunt?" Savage asked.

"Not her ass or her junk," Fritz giggled, "at least not anymore. They were worse than anyone in my family, by far! And we're real animals when it comes to that sort of thing."

Jamie shook his head to clear it, and locked eyes with Lulu on the other side of a dining table. She was licking her lips like her favorite snack was hot and ready in front of her. Jamie blinked, then held his eyes closed and turned his head. The sensations washed over him, like feeling the aura of static electricity when touching a plasma ball.

"North," he said, turning his head in that direction, his eyes still closed. "I feel, almost smell, the energies that the Professor was using at the University, pulsing in the north. I can lead us there."

"Good," Croaker said. "Keep your eyes closed and your hands in plain view. Markus, lead the way to our new transportation. We've got somewhere to be."

"I hope they have food," Fritz said. "I'm starving."

Travis I. Sivart

10. Riders on the Storm

Byron climbed behind the wheel of the antique car that reminded him of his childhood. It was a vintage station wagon, with all the bells and whistles, including wood paneling along the sides, no seat belts in the back, and a rear facing third row seat. He remembered going to the drive-in theater in the last millennia—more than half a century ago—and wrapping himself in a quilt his grandmother had made. It smelled of dog, cigarettes, and greasy popcorn.

Fritz slammed the door in the back seat, breaking Bryon out of his reverie. Kitty settled into the front passenger seat and Jamie and Croaker climbed into the back.

"Trade places with me," Haunt said, elbowing Fritz. "I don't want to sit on the hump, and you're smaller."

"Just because I'm small doesn't mean I should get the middle," Fritz muttered. "But if we get shot at, then a window seat will be the first person to get hit, so okay, let's switch!"

The two men changed places, Fritz climbing over Haunt as Byron shifted into reverse on the steering column and backed out of the parking space. Once out of the garage, they swung into the evening's rush hour traffic, rain pelting the windshield.

"That way," Haunt leaned forward, his arm jutting across the front seat and pointing at the next road. "I can almost taste them. They're doing something big and it's making my scalp prickle like a hedgehog on cocaine."

"Weird comparison," Croaker said, "but okay. Who are they?"

Byron glanced into the rearview mirror and saw the Haunt's face pucker. He couldn't tell if it was in distaste or concentration.

His facial readings say it's from nervous reaction, boss, Jordan said in Byron's head. *And yes, I have completely rebooted and am back online. I'm sending a map to your HUD, tracking where we are, and projecting a path using Jamie's directions.*

"I'm not sure," the Haunt continued, his eyes closed and his chin lifted as he scented the air. "But it's big, I know that. I can feel something like what was in the uni. But that was like smelling a distant favorite restaurant, like the ginger and garlic of your favorite Asian food. This is like being sprayed in the face with old lady perfume. It's cloying and makes me want to gag."

"You're scenting the air," Fritz said, raising his nose and breathing deep. "I have a super sniffer, but don't smell anything other than your body odor, the alcohol on Croaker, the fact that Kitty is on her period…"

"Hey!" Kitty interrupted. "No need to announce it."

"No, it's okay, I don't mind," Fritz continued, "but it is off. Is that because of your cybernetics?"

"Personal much?" Kitty turned to glare at Fritz. "But yes, the bio-mechanical components messed with my hormones, so everything is out of whack. And no, that doesn't explain my moods. I'm just naturally intense."

Byron followed Haunt's directions, ignoring the conversation as Jordan continued feeding him information.

The authorities have yet to pick up on any disturbance in the area, Jordan said, *but I am tracking an atmospheric electromagnetic disturbance in the direction we're heading. It seems to either be feeding the storm or feeding off it. The local police have not been notified of us or the missing vehicle.*

"Either the T.A.L.O.N. Agency is still busy with their emotional breakdown," Byron informed the others, "or they're keeping it quiet."

"So they don't cause a panic?" Kitty asked.

"More likely it's so they get to whatever is happening before anyone else and get first pick of the spoils," Croaker said.

"The world's gone to shit," Byron growled. "Ghosts, werewolves, and other things are out there now. I suspect they've always been there, but something happened recently that opened up some sort of door and let a lot more into the world."

"You know what happened," Croaker said, looking into Bryon's eyes in the rearview. "You've met Silver and the Hawk, and I'm pretty sure you did your homework on them."

"This is a technological world," Kitty injected, "and we shouldn't be dealing with the supernatural."

"Too late for that, sweet cakes," Haunt said, pointing at the highway entrance. "Get on the highway. That'll be the fastest route to where we need to go."

The sky in the distance opened up, the clouds parting in a swirl. Byron stared at the center, where a darker cloud rotated in the opposite direction, green lightning arcing through it. Something massive moved within the middle, dark lines reaching for the ground below.

That's it, boss, Jordan said in Byron's ear. *Head for that. And it looks like it's directly over the Eye in the Sky theme park.*

"The Eye in the Sky theme park?" Byron said aloud.

"What?" Fritz leaned over the front seat, tilting his head to look up at the clouds. "That place was closed for renovations earlier this year. Massive reworking of rides using graphene for power sources, now that it's cheaper since Jones Industries went under and no longer have a corner on that market."

"More than that," Haunt said, wincing, "that's where my

headache is coming from. But good news, my emotional demon has returned. And it's hungry for the smorgasbord of energy coming from that cloud."

Ten minutes later, they pulled off the exit for the park, turning up the two-lane road leading to the front gates. An intricate wrought-iron gate arced above the road. Odd creatures in the throes of a torrid dance decorated the arch, showing a horror theme to the park within. Empty guard booths stood beside the six lanes leading to the multi-acre parking lots.

Byron guided the station wagon towards the main gates, leaning forward to watch the tendrils reaching down from the heavens. Black spinning columns touched the earth and dragged thick tentacles across the islands of grass and leafless trees, uprooting the hibernating plants and pulling them back into the clouds.

The park entrance was a series of covered, empty ticket booths and beyond them were whirling rides with neon lights. A Ferris wheel spun, showing deserted cars spinning in an endless circle with a bloodshot eye in the center. A tilt-a-whirl spun frantically to one side beyond the medieval castle-like structures of shops and food stands. Ropey strands of light shot into the sky, creating standalone whirlwinds of entertainment; if they were intertwined with a nightmare.

Music drifted from the park, a cacophony of tinny sounds mixing with the deep thumping bass of electronic AI-created compositions. Smells of sickly sweet cotton candy competed with the scent of grilling meats and the wispier aroma of baked treats.

The perimeter fence, three meters high, pulsed with a rhythmic light as it ran through the entirety of the metal barrier. Bursts of sparks erupted at the intersection of the exterior and interior fences.

Pulling up to the curb outside of the entrance, the five piled out of the car. They assembled on the sidewalk, staring up at the growing tempest above, and Byron shrugged.

Snapping his mag-pulse open on his wrist, he drew his firearm with his free hand. Behind him and to the right, Kitty powered up her arm and her vibro-whip flicked to life in her other hand. On Byron's left, Croaker muttered as he watched the tendril-ridden storm, digging into his coat and satchel and snapping miscellaneous gadgets together until he held an oversized rifle with whirring gears, hissing pressure gauges, and clicking apparatus in both hands. Behind the three, Fritz growled, tugging at the collar of the gray sweatsuit he'd picked up from the trunk of spare clothing back at the Midnight Progeny hideout. Haunt stood a little further out on the opposite side, pulling his sleeve cuffs out of the bomber jacket he'd acquired after discarding his fancy suit jacket.

"I don't think I need to say it," Haunt said, "but there's some massive-ass supernatural activity here. My elemental is going crazy. She's jerking at her bond to me like a bloodhound ready to take down her quarry."

"Yah think?" Fritz said, sweat beading on his forehead and flexing his hands. "This is the first time I think I've felt like we've had anything in common."

"I'm guessing we're heading for the center of the park?" Byron asked.

"Yeah," Haunt nodded, "that's what I'm picking up."

"My super-sniffer says the same," Fritz agreed.

"Yeah," Croaker nodded, checking a gauge on his cobbled weapon. "Looks like I'm seeing the same."

Without discussion, the wedge of five moved forward, the wind whipping through their various coats and rippling their hair. They passed the ticket stands, climbed over the locked turnstiles, and started down the main thoroughfare.

Half-built animatronics turned to watch their progress, gears whirring and naked mechanisms clicking. The mascots of the park shifted in place, smaller mechanical spider-like constructs darting through the low shadows, snatching as tumbling leaves and errant scraps of papers.

"They're following us," Kitty murmured. "The fracking

things are creepy, but they're probably just following their programming to interact with the guests."

They moved through the gathering gloom—neon and LED cutting through the mists rolling across the ground—and followed the meandering path towards the center of the park. The rides whirred and whizzed, music stuttering and speeding up as they passed. The seven immense rollers coasters on the outskirts of the park rattled and roared, speakers blaring exciting music and imitation screams of thrill-seekers.

The entire park was built in the shape of an eye. The outer circle of the sclera held the coasters, the iris was a ring of shops and eateries, and the pupil held the gem of the park. The Vortex, a cylindrical tower that rose dozens of stories into the sky like a shard of broken technology and crystal was the centerpiece. It was a wonder of modern advancements, completely self-sufficient for energy and housing a half-dozen attractions within it.

Above it was the literal eye of the storm. An optical orb larger than a shopping mall shifted back and forth above the theme park, darting with a panicked shifting. Three stories above the ground stood Professor Elmo on a balcony, surrounded by scurrying forms of darkness. The man stood with his arms raised to the storm, chanting in a foreign tongue, the words ripped away by the winds.

"Sumerian," Byron said. "My AI says he's speaking ancient Sumerian, but can't pick it up clearly."

"What are we here to do?" Kitty asked. "I mean, I know we need to fracking stop him, but how? Do we have a license to kill? Can I just put one between his eyes and call it a day?"

"Sure, kid," Croaker said, "give it a shot. Pun intended."

Kitty raised her arm and aimed along the cannon. Her arm jerked and a streak of energy shot into the night. The man on the balcony exploded, white lab coat and crazy hair flying in all directions. Kitty lowered her arm.

"That was easy," she smiled, sounding more chipper

than she had the entire mission.

A click of metal on concrete came from behind the group, followed by dozens more of similar sounds. Turning as one, they saw the haphazard animatronic creations from the entrance creeping from the shadows between buildings and attractions, dozens and dozens of trash-collecting spiders scurrying around their legs.

"Um," Kitty looked Croaker, "shouldn't killing him have stopped all these other things?"

"Maybe we need to take out the park's power source?" Byron suggested.

"Or kill the huge thing in the sky above us?" Haunt added, his voice husky.

The sound of nails on a chalkboard filled the air, a shrill scream of intense pain and anger, and a muted thwump came from the balcony above them where the professor had been moments before.

"Oh, shit," Byron said, his HUD zooming in to the empty space where Professor Elmo had disappeared.

He watched as scraps of cloth, flesh, bloody body parts, and purplish energy congealed on the balcony until an obscene mockery of the man stood where the professor had been moments ago. The being had three arms—an extra one with long claws jutting from the center of his back and thrusting above his head—thick, dark green legs with pulsing veins, and a patchwork hooded cloak of red-tinted cloth tatters. Elmo's head raised towards the roiling mass above the park and slowly turned to look directly at the group.

The man had a large, single green eye with phlegm-colored veins within, no nose, and a mouth filled with jagged teeth that went from one pointed ear to the other. It grinned, then looked up, and a torrent of purplish energy erupted upwards, piercing the cloud cover. Another eye in the dark clouds opened and shifted towards the small group on the ground.

11. Inn to the Deep

Wanderly whistled quietly to himself, tapping his fingertips against the table to keep the rhythm. This was something he did when working through a problem. The idea someone was gunning for Jack was stuck in the small man's head, and he turned away from the wide viewscreen.

Everyone else in the room stared, transfixed by the events unfolding as the man on the balcony exploded and reformed, calling down the attention of dozens of eyes in the stormy sky overhead. Even Cogsley and Golem had stopped their tasks and watched, unable to tear themselves away.

Wanderly grabbed his gin and tonic, scooted out of the booth across from Nomed, and pattered across the floor. He needed to pace, to think, to work out this thing niggling at the edges of his brain. Sipping at his drink, he weaved between the tables at the edge of the dance floor and made his way behind the bar.

Once upon a time, this was his place. Before Cogsley was around, even before Jack came home to roost and make the travelling tavern his place of residence. Now, Jack spent all his time here. It was almost like he was afraid to leave. Sure, he said that he'd made a vow to not directly interfere anymore, but he never said why.

Well, that wasn't completely true.

Jack said he made the vow because he broke the world. But he never said how he did that.

Wanderly had known the man for a long time. After the halfling had lived a very full and interesting life as an adventurer, he'd settled here. But back then, here was a massive machine. A submarine, to be specific. It had ever-changing and shifting rooms and moved through time and space—like outer space—the way a regular submersible would travel through water.

Thinking about his adventuring days, Wanderly smiled, still whistling, remembering the time he'd whistled up a hurricane. *Lots of hurricane references were happening today,* he thought. *That was shortly before the events that birthed Nomed and freed Verl'zen-luk to become a god. Or was it after? It's hard to remember what order things happened in, once time is no longer a linear concept.*

For example, Byron Savage was someone I hung out with just a few months ago. But the cyborg was hundreds of years old when that happened. Right now he was only…what, fifty? Seventy? Whatever he was, he was in his prime, and the world he knew hadn't been shattered yet.

"I need to go somewhere…" Wanderly muttered, wondering if anyone else ever felt like that. Wondering if other people had a strange urge to leave, that they were supposed to be somewhere else, doing something that they couldn't quite put their finger on. "I need to do Laundry."

Laundry? He thought. *Wasn't that where Byron had met Grandma, Moots, Gina, and Nahla before they came into the tavern? And why was it called the Traveller's Inn? It was really more of a pub or a nightclub. But…it did always have rooms available to the select few.*

Even now, Wanderly was staring up a back stairway leading to rooms to let. He looked down at his arm and noticed his hand was on a door latch. One he didn't recognize. The inn still constantly rearranged itself, but it never had a basement before, had it? When it was a submersible, it had the lower decks where the machinery that powered it lay hidden. He remembered it well. He'd done something very important there once. But couldn't quite recall what it had been.

The door was open now, and he still held the knob in his hand, the door swaying back and forth in front of him. Hadn't it been a latch a moment ago? *It doesn't matter; the inn changes when the inn wants to change.* Shrugging, Wanderly took another drink from his glass and wobbled forward into the darkness. He set his foot on the top step leading down to the basement, let go of the door, and stumbled. His hand shot out, grabbing the railing, and the door slammed behind him.

He paused, getting his balance and taking another sip from his drink, waiting for his eyes to adjust. The bit of light from under the door showed the stairs leading down.

"Wanderly," a familiar voice in the inky blankness below said, "it's good to see you again. Come on down, let's talk about what I've missed."

Jack hit the pause button, and the small crowd in the room moaned in disappointment.

"Come on, Jack," Mogits said, standing to stretch, "it just got to the exciting part!"

Sam and the others echoed the sentiment in a chorus of complaints, but Jack held up a finger, tilted his head, and listened.

"What is it, Jack?" Tiffene said from his elbow, making him jump.

"Maybe he felt the shift?" Manx suggested, looking up from the music box he was tinkering with.

"No," Jack shook his head, then stopped to look at the others around him. "Mogits? Manx? Sam? Tiffene? When did you four get here?"

"Oooh, Jack, what're you talking about?" Sam growled. "We've been here the whole time."

Sam waved a hand towards the room, and the gathered crowd nodded agreement. All except Nomed, who tilted his head and squinted at Jack.

"Okay, everyone," Jack raised his voice to be heard, "we're going to take a quick break, then pick up where we left off. Nomed, can I talk to you over here?"

Jack set down the remote and stepped to a dark corner and waited for Nomed to join him. He watched the demon-kin throw back his drink, raise the glass to Golem for a refill, then head to where Jack stood.

"What's up, Jack?" Nomed asked, crossing his arms.

"Something changed," Jack said hesitantly, looking past the man. "Did you notice it?"

"Notice it?" Nomed glanced behind him at the others, then returned his gaze to Jack and shook his head. "But I felt something. Couldn't say what it was, but something weird…different happened. Do you know what it is?"

"No," Jack breathed, "but I'm glad I wasn't the only one. Do you remember Mogits and the others being here the entire time? And where's Wanderly?"

The two men turned and surveyed the room. Cogsley was setting a fresh drink on Nomed's table. Elementius was leaning in to Tilbert, pointing at something on the running transcript scrolling from his machine. Golem FloorSweeper was nowhere to be seen, but Durg and Darome were in their usual spots at the bar.

"Wanderly was at the table a few minutes ago," Nomed pointed at the empty bench, "and Tiffene, Sam, Manx, and…" Nomed trailed off, shaking his head. "I think they were here, but I don't remember them being part of the conversation. I mean, you specifically called on everyone in the place to get their input a little while ago, and I don't recall them saying anything."

"Right," Jack nodded, "and there are new doors. In fact, that entire wall is different. Were there vintage video games along the wall the last time you looked?"

Nomed stared at the ancient screens showing Pac-man, Donkey Kong, and Space Invaders.

"Jack," he said, "what's going on? I thought you controlled what shifted and changed in this place."

"So, you know about that, then?" Jack asked.

"Some of us do," Nomed shrugged. "Wanderly because of his little chaos circuit, me because of mine, and I think Elementius and Tilbert usually notice because they keep themselves apart from the actual events in the Tavern…"

"Wait," Jack interrupted, "tavern?"

"Well, yeah," Nomed shrugged again. "I mean, it's called the Traveller's Inn—a play on you being the Traveller, and the fact that you are in the house at the moment—but let's face it, it's more of a tavern than an inn. The rooms are secondary to the rooms you let people stay in without ever charging them."

"Interesting," Jack mumbled. "When did that shift happen?"

"Is that rhetorical, Jack?" Nomed grinned, looking at Jack. "It's been more of a classic meet-up pub than an overnight stay for most of its existence."

The two fell silent, observing the room. Then Jack sighed, threw up his hands and shook his head.

"Well, we can't change the name now," Jack said, "but we can agree that the Tavern has a welcoming feel. But I still want to know, where is Wanderly? Did he go through one of the new doors? Like you said, I usually know when changes happen. But now, there's a bunch of doors I don't remember appearing. There's the one to a new bathroom, that one leading to a second bar, and the one to the basement-"

"Basement?" Nomed dropped a hand to Jack's wrist, stopping the other man from gesturing. "Since when does the inn have a basement?"

"Since always…" the words slowed as Jack said them. "But it hadn't been around for, well, for a long time. What brought the basement back?"

"And do you think," Nomed looked at Jack, "that Wanderly went down there?"

"Are you suggesting," Jack returned Nomed's concerned look, "that you didn't notice Wanderly—the loudest, most flamboyant, and most talkative of anyone in the Traveller's Inn—got up from your table, moved across a crowded room, and went through a door that's plainly obvious, with no one noticing? Not even you, with your paranoia and penchant for noticing things? Not even me, who feels every shift in this building?"

"He was the landlord before you showed up and took charge of the place, right?" Nomed asked.

"Yeah," Jack sighed, "he was. And he has a connection to the place. I called it into existence but put him in as a placeholder until I could come and take charge."

"And you showed up after you did something that you deemed so important and destructive," Nomed said slowly, "that you decided to stay in this place and not directly interfere ever again?"

"Well, I wouldn't say ever again," Jack gruffed, "just not for a while, until I fixed my screw up."

"And do you normally hide from your problems, Jack?" Nomed asked. "Do you normally let everyone else go into the danger and fight your battles?"

"I'm not sure what you're getting at, Nomed," Jack said, scrunching up his brow. "What's your point?"

"Remember the benefactor we mentioned before?" Nomed asked, and Jack nodded. "Perhaps they're not a benefactor, but a manipulator. Like me. A malefactor, and someone who's looking to take what you have."

The two men jumped as the screen blared back to life, Mogits standing and holding the remote as the world beyond the screen erupted in flames.

The Traveller's Inn

97

12. The SciFi Five

Croaker watched the man-turned-monstrosity grin at the heavens, his mouth splitting vertically, as well as horizontally, and the noise coming from it sounded like a thousand seals being tortured by a thousand gargling leprechauns. The various rides and attractions around the park sprung to life, whirling and whizzing, music filling the air in a chaotic cornucopia cacophony of mindless metallic madness.

Waterspouts rose on the mighty Mississippi River on the eastern border of the park, spraying a fine mist over the scene that settled to the ground as a thick fog. Small animals screeched and scurried from bushes into the flashing lights, turning gleaming eyes up towards the thing in the clouds. The bulbs along the perimeter fence twinkled in rhythm, creating a spiraling effect around the entire park with the Vortex at the center.

Croaker looked around at his companions, fumbling at his satchel with one hand and cradling his cobbled together weapon with the other. They'd turned away from one another, forming a circle pointing outward. Kitty jerked her vibro-dagger from its sheath and it hummed to life, her whip echoing the noise as it rattled and sparked on the asphalt at the end of her arm cannon. Haunt was half crouched, his arms spread wide and a feral look on his face. A pale blue form hovered over the man's shoulder, mimicking his movements, but its ethereal head turning to look at Croaker. Savage faced the way they'd come from, his pistol held up beside his head as he sighted down the V of his mag-pulse. Fritz surprised Croaker the most. The small man was growling deep in his throat, hooked fingers ripped at his sweat suit, tearing it from his chest. Hair sprouted from the man's back, and his ears grew to points.

A noise from the shadows drew Croaker's attention. Animatronics lumbered forward in hurky-jerky motions, heads tilting to stare at the group through backlit eyes with no eyelids. The small trash spiders darted around the feet of their larger counterparts, grabbing at anything within reach and stuffing it into the clicking, clattering mandibles on the front of their rounded, metallic bodies.

The abomination that was once Elmo raised his three arms and howled again, streaks of purple energy jumping from the tower to him as he redirected the flow towards the ground.

"Scatter!" Croaker yelled, limping away at top speed.

The others looked up and saw the arcs of St. Elmo's fire from the transformed professor shoot downward and hit two animatronic creatures. The machines lurched into a higher gear, lumbering forward. Savage fired his pistol at one, hitting it. It turned towards him, unaffected by his blasts.

"Aw, crap," Savage muttered, holstering his pistol and drawing a stun baton.

Moving forward, he swung at the thing's head. His baton sparked as it made contact, and Savage was thrown backwards as the energy rebounded. Kitty was there then, standing over him. Her vibro-whip lashed out, cutting through the metal arm of the construct.

A dozen of the small trash spiders darted forward and Fritz leapt into the middle of them. The man was covered from head to toe with puffy orangish-red fur, small ears perked forward. He'd transformed from human to a were-beast that resembled a two-legged Pomeranian, black claws slashing, barking in high-pitched bursts. He tore into the machines, tearing them apart and throwing wiggling legs and bulbous bodies around.

Croaker looked at the attachment he'd pulled out of his satchel and worked it into his weapon. A streak of blue and Haunt's scream caught his attention. The ghostly being that had been hovering over the psychic no longer looked like a gentlewoman from a bygone age, and had transformed into exactly what Croaker thought a banshee would look like. Tattered and torn cloth streamed behind the elongated form as she dove into one of the larger constructs, and the machine froze, jittering in place.

Turning away from the surrounding fight, Croaker kneeled, set his rifle to his shoulder, and aimed at the thing that was once the professor. Gears whirred and steam hissed as Croaker pulled the trigger. A dozen small, spiked pellets flew forward, pelting the creature and embedding into its rubbery flesh, then exploded.

Croaker didn't see the result; a two-meter tall, mouse-like construct barreled into him, knocking him to the ground. A handful of the spider-bots scurried across him, pincers tearing at his coat and face. Crab-crawling backwards, Croaker dropped his gun and pulled the small bots off his body, leaving a network of scratches amidst chunks of missing flesh.

Fritz was on him a moment later, attacking the trash machines, while Kitty screeched a war cry as her vibro-whip slashed and slapped at the larger animatronic above Croaker. The older man scrambled for his dropped weapon, looking up and over his shoulder towards the man directing the battle from three-stories up.

Elmo was a mess. One arm hung, useless, by his side, and another scraped at his face. One of his thick, green legs had a hole large enough to put a fist into, and his bifurcated mouth hung awkwardly on one side.

Croaker's mind frantically ran through options. Shutting down the mad scientist should break the cycle and stop all the park attractions from killing them and potentially taking over the world.

Grabbing his weapon, Croaker pushed to his feet under the protest of his aged knees. Fritz darted across his path, teeth barred and throwing small mechanical critters in all directions. Kitty blocked the incoming animatronics, dagger flashing and whip cracking.

"How do we get to that bastard?" Croaker muttered, backpedaling and holding on to his fedora as he directed his eyes upward.

"I can do that," Haunt said from behind Croaker, thrusting a hand with fingers splayed over the older man's shoulder.

A dozen wispy forms launched forward, swirling around one another and crashing into the man on the balcony. Elmo stumbled backwards, throwing his hands up and screaming. His broken jaw fell, tumbling down the side of the building and smashing on the asphalt at Croaker's feet.

"Haunt," Croaker pointed at the shattered mandible, "can you use that as a focus? A physical part of your target to help your spirits get him?"

"Fracking metaphysical mumbo-jumbo!" Savage shouted. "How about a few of these instead?"

Sidestepping, Croaker moved out of the cyborg's line of fire as the man raised his mag-pulse and his arm jerked repeatedly.

Croaker had seen this man work, but only in vids. He'd had reports from his clients, Silver and Smith, telling about Byron Savage's personal code of honor. He'd even considered contacting Savage to see if he needed a finder to hook him up with new clients and cases. But to see him in action, first person, was a different thing altogether.

"Kitty," Savage shouted, "let's climb and bring it to him!"

Savage leapt straight up, grabbing the protruding outcroppings of the Vortex tower and launching himself further. Kitty followed his example, but with a gymnast's grace, flipping and spinning from handhold to beam to bar until she landed next to Savage on the balcony above the main fray. The spirits that Haunt summoned still harangued the man, and Savage's punch in the man's midsection bent him double. Kitty spun and planted a foot in the man's shattered face.

Croaker recovered his weapon and looked around at the remaining fray on the ground level. Fritz had torn through most of the trash collecting spiders, but a dozen animatronics still lumbered forward.

"Haunt," Croaker pointed with his makeshift rifle, "behind us, incoming! Fritz, get on the big guys and shut them down!"

Firing into the technological horrors, Croaker was satisfied: his weapon's electrical setting pulled from the surrounding lights and mechanisms, frying the circuitry of the enemy. But there were so many, and he could only target one at a time.

Fritz leapt a half-dozen meters through the air and landed on the shoulders of the machine reaching for Croaker, tearing its arms from its sockets and beating the machine with its own appendages. The blue demon spirit that raged over Haunt's head surged forward and slammed into another animatronic.

The machine jittered, its red eyes fading to a purple. It reoriented towards its allies and punched one in the face. The mechanical form stumbled backwards, its head tearing from its shoulders. The possessed machine jerked and flashed, then exploded in a shower of sparks as it collapsed.

"Beings from other worlds," Haunt said, shrugging, "have been playing havoc with our technology since we invented it. They can't control them for long, but they can mess them up lickity split!"

"You and Fritz have these guys under control," Croaker

said, firing another shot into an attacker and looking up at the balcony, "let's hope Kitty and Savage are doing as well."

Above the battleground, the two street samurai were in full engagement with the leader of the enemy. Elmo's third arm held Savage off the ground by his bald head, and Kitty lashed at the enemy's exposed legs with her vibro-whip. Croaker took aim, swinging the muzzle of his contraption left and right, trying to get a clear shot.

Purplish energy exploded from the Doctor-Professor, throwing Kitty backwards into open air. Fritz surged upward, leaping to his full ability, snatching the woman from her plummet in mid-air. The were-Pomeranian landed on his feet and gave the street samurai a toothy grin.

The abomination's two free arms grabbed at Savage's head, tearing at the flesh over metal, pulling at anything it could get a hold of. Savage aimed both feet, swinging back towards the Professor-Doctor and sunk into the man's chest. Gore burst into a speckled array of mist, lights of the surrounding rides turning it into a spectacular display. Ribs erupted through the flesh and Savage fell backwards, his back hitting the railing and his torso hanging in the open air.

Croaker took the shot. His weapon jerked, throwing his shoulder back, but the explosive pellets flew true, striking Elmo in his shoulders and head. Savage's feet tore free of the man's torso and he tumbled head over teakettle past the railing. Twisting as he fell, Savage turned around and landed with a sidewalk cracking thud. Chunks of bloody flesh and muscle rained down around the group as the bits of the Professor hit the ground.

"Let the bodies hit the floor," Fritz giggled, "is the same song as It's Raining Men, but from a different point of view."

"Ew," Kitty sighed, "and put me down puppy-boy."

Fritz set the woman on her feet, smiling at her with his tongue lolling out of the side of his extended muzzle.

"You're kinda cute like this," Kitty said, rumpling the fur on Fritz's head.

"Yah, I know," Fritz grinned, "but am I cute enough for a belly rubs later?"

"Maybe," Kitty giggled, blushing, "but no. Stop looking at me like that. OMG, this is so awkward!"

"Did we win?" Savage asked, his voice gravel in a concrete mixer. "Or do we still need to break some heads?"

"Um, well," Croaker hemmed, looking around. "That depends. Is that thing in the sky eyeballing us, or is it retreating?"

Everyone looked up, then around them. The animatronic attackers lay scattered across the sidewalk, intermixed with the trash spiders, twitching and sparking. Above them, the massive dark form in the center of the spiraling clouds opened a dozen eyes. Each threw a spotlight across the park, and the waterspouts on the river collapsed.

The sound of wet, slapping footsteps came from the thick fog surrounding the group, and the thing above them blinked.

13. Science vs. Religion

Kitty's arm cannon was dead, but her vibro-whip and dagger still had power. She saw Croaker, her mentor and father figure, fumbling at his satchel and gun. He was trying to adapt his weapon to take on this new foe. He always tried to protect others, all while complaining what idiots they were for not being prepared. She felt that right now, but also knew he was never prepared either. He was just more prepared to *adapt* than others.

Kitty took stock again, determined to not need help this time. It was embarrassing that the damned puppy-guy had caught her. She would've landed fine, and maybe not even broken her legs. She was enhanced after all, but it was mostly upper body and nerves. She could react seventy percent faster than trained athletes, but it didn't mean her bones wouldn't break when she fell from three stories up.

The icky thing in the sky no longer had one huge eyeball staring at them. Instead, it had a dozen smaller ones that flew around in the cloud above. Each focused on something different, and Kitty couldn't tell if they were each attached to the larger creature, or operating independently. Figures moved in the fog at the edge of the clearing they'd created around the Vortex tower in the middle of the park.

"Eye in the Sky theme park," Kitty laughed ruefully. "It's taken on such a creepy, literal meaning, hasn't it?"

"It's okay," Fritz patted her arm reassuringly. "I'll make this thing my bitch."

Looking down at the smaller man, Kitty took in his appearance completely for the first time since she'd last seen him. He was still the same height, not quite reaching her shoulder. But he was no longer human. He was like a werewolf, but a thousand times cuter with a puffy, rounded head, orange fur, and perky ears. His tongue flopped out of the side of his muzzle, and his deep brown eyes stared up at her adoringly. Had he always looked at her that way?

She did kinda want to give him a belly rub. And scrub behind his ears. She wanted to see if he'd do that leg thing if she did. Then she saw the bright, safety-orange speedo he wore. She didn't know how to feel about that. On one hand, so sexy. On the other hand, he was a meter-and-a-half tall, fluffy killing machine in a speedo.

She wondered briefly if that would be good for her, or self-destructive. She avoided getting close to people, not to protect herself, but to protect them. Of course, trusting people was something her father and upbringing had broken her of. Though Croaker helped show her it could be okay. Sometimes.

"Heads up, people!" Croaker shouted, bringing her attention back to the situation. He jabbed his weapon towards the sky, but his free hand indicated the moving shadows at the edge of the asphalt clearing.

Kitty's nerves tingled, enhanced by her biometrics. Unlike Savage, she didn't have the nanotechnology that interacted with her nervous system and attached to her blood cells. Hers specifically focused on heightening her brain to muscle reaction algorithm. She was elite and epic when it came to targeting nerve clusters and pressure points, enhancing her reaction times and agility. She may not be able to jump to a roof in a single bound, but she could get to a roof using gymnastics beyond any normal human's ability. She'd never take someone out in a single punch, but she could paralyze them with two hits and take them out with a series of strategic strikes along their nervous system.

Turning towards the army of figures emerging through the fog, she pinpointed the possible strike points of the fish-men, then stopped. They were fracking fish people! The same sort of humanoids from the laboratory!

"You bastards may have gotten the best of me before," she muttered, "but I'm ready for you this time. This is my turf, not some weird science lab when I can't pick you out."

The whirring lights around the perimeter of the park accelerated, blending into a blur of sight and sound as a thick tentacle crashed to the ground between Kitty and her target. She backpedaled, trying to regain her equilibrium.

Fritz shot past her, latching onto the rubbery appendage and climbing, tearing chunks of flesh as he rose into the night. Savage opened fire, targeting the fish-men surging forward. Croaker removed attachments from his rifle, replacing them with tubes and gauges, adjusting his weapon to a better configuration. The first blast from the firearm ripped through a thick, alien tendril that flopped to the ground. It writhed and lashed out, breaking the Vortex tower where Elmo had been.

The structure creaked, leaning towards Kitty, and tumbling in an elongated wreckage that was the mechanical equivalent of the monstrosities' appendages in the sky. Kitty dove to the side in a somersault, coming up on her feet and lashing out with her vibro-whip as another tentacle reached for her. It wrapped around an ice-cream cart next to her and drew it upward, crushing it. Small metal pieces rained down.

"How the hell do we stop a thing in the sky?" Kitty muttered. "We can't reach it, and it can crush metal on a whim!"

"We get them from the inside then," came a hissing voice from beside her. Haunt was staring up into the sky, his eyes wide and wild. He slowly raised a hand, exhaustion showing in his movements, and three ethereal forms darted past, penetrating the being in the center of one of the dozen thick stalks scraping the ground. "Go my beauties. Find the heart and mind and destroy everything you touch."

Kitty felt a mix of emotions tear through her. On one hand, great! Ghosts invading the alien invader. On the other hand, how icky was it that this man sent ghosts to attack someone's mind? Even something that never belonged in the world shouldn't go through that.

That thought gave Kitty pause. If this thing didn't belong here, then maybe it missed something important to how things worked in this world or reality. She looked up, along the trailing stalk dragging the ground in front of her, and focused on the beak-like protrusion gaping in the center of the rotating storm.

Kitty ran forward and jumped. Grabbing a sucker-like protrusion, she propelled herself upward. Staring towards her goal, she launched herself again, concerned cries following her progress. Croaker roared an objection at his protégé, firing his weapon into the shambling horde of web-fingered and toed creatures shuffling towards him and the others. Fritz jumped from enemy to enemy, his wounds healing at an unnatural rate as he shredded flesh and scale. Savage stood stoically, firing his laser pistol into enemies and battered skulls and bodies with his stun baton. Haunt screamed as his ghostly counterparts fed on his energy to power their existence, throwing everything he had into his demonic companion and minions to save the world.

Continuing her climb, the sounds of the battle below faded. She'd always wanted to be a hero, but she'd never thought it would happen like this. In her head, it had always been in a deadly showdown in the center of a city street, buildings rising on either side in an urban canyon. Or slinking through a warehouse, taking down a group of gangsters hiding in the shadows amidst crates and steaming pipes. It almost always ended with her flying into a rage and running at her enemies, terror in their eyes as she mowed them down with her particularly violent skill set.

Kitty never imagined it like this. Climbing a sticky, gooey, slippery appendage of some sort of extra-dimensional alien the size of a corporate mega-plex. It also never took place after she'd used all three shots stored in her forearm laser auto-cannon. That left her with…what? A vibro-whip and dagger? She doubted cutting up a gigantic squid tentacle would kill this thing. Not when it had dozens more trailing from the immense, cloud-covered form hovering a couple hundred meters above the ground.

Reaching the edge of the turbulent clouds, Kitty gave one last look at the panoramic view of the battle below. Kitty's friends were in a row, facing the flailing line of fiendish freaks on the riverside and a broken line of mechanical monstrosities on the other side. She wished for Savage's ocular enhancements so she could zoom in and take a last look at her team.

She picked Croaker's tiny form out of the chaos, launching something from his modified rifle. The small disks whizzed through the air and stuck to various tentacles of the sky-bound horror. Savage and Fritz were facing down the advancing crowd of enemies, the former firing his pistol at point blank range and punching through his targets. Fritz was an orange blur, flying from one foe to another, tearing them to pieces. But there were so many, there were always two more to replace any that fell.

Haunt stood in the center, his pale face looking up. Not at her. He stared at the writhing mass above her, his arms flailing like he was blindly throwing things into the sky. Ghostly forms whirled past her, zipping into the center of the spiraling dance of tentacles and cumulonimbus cover overhead.

The edge of the theme park was a swirl of lights and color of the centrifuge of the massive hadron collider built into the perimeter. She needed to stop this thing in the sky, and that should interrupt the power of the machine below, closing the rift between her world and wherever this thing came from.

Kitty turned back to her objective and climbed the last few meters into the thick, dark, moist mist. Madness ensued. She felt her mind shudder as dozens of eyes appeared in the fog. Not pairs of eyes, like she thought she should see, but individual orbs ranging in size from a tennis ball to a beach ball. Riptides of wind currents tugged at her, the way the insanity pulled at her brain. Ethereal forms darted around the eyes—*Haunt's minions*, she guessed—disappearing and reappearing from the fog and the free-floating orbs.

She leapt from the massive trunk she'd climbed and threw herself into the murk, landing on an eyeball and jumping again. Her foot sank into the orb, and it blinked without the aid of an eyelid. Kitty's mind slipped a little further.

Then she was standing on a soft, swampy surface, mist crawling across her feet and creeping up her legs in thin wisps. Her nerves screamed out as cold crept into where they touched, numbing her. Her consciousness tumbled through scenarios. For a moment, she was on an alien planet in a space suit. Then she was slogging through the knee-deep dust of a volcanic wasteland. When the imagery of a sinking ship crossed her mind, she locked onto it, solidifying the hallucinations into something she could understand.

She was on the deck of a waterlogged ship, her feet sinking into the boards, and she took a step forward, pulling her boots free of the mystical mire. The hovering, glowing orbs were floating above the deck, thin silvery cords extending from their forms to a shadowy figure in the mist. The being lurched forward, appearing awkward as it walked, as if unused to it.

Emerging from the murk came a genderless being, topped by a head that looked more like a squid than anything else. Torn and tattered seventeenth century pirate regalia draped across the rest of the figure. A wicked, saw-toothed blade shimmered in one hand, and a hook adorned the other.

"You," came the gurgle of a voice, "have chosen the

form of your death. We shall devour and absorb you into ourselves. Prepare yourself to be boarded and looted of your individuality…"

Kitty didn't wait for the thing to finish speaking. She charged forward, her vibro-ship snapping forward like a magical lash connected to her mind. Her vibro-dagger followed, slicing across the invader's midsection. Both glowed like magical weapons from a fantasy novel, leaving glittering silver trails in their wake. This was Kitty's showdown. Her rage-fantasy turned into reality, and she wasn't going to miss the opportunity her mind had craved for so long.

Wisps of vengeful souls swirled around her, and she recognized the spirits that Haunt sent into the cloud. The fragmented essences burst around Kitty and darted towards the surrounding optical orbs of the enemy, enveloping and engaging them. Kitty felt the being in front of her shrink into itself as its support system was attacked.

Leaning into her offensive, Kitty jerked her glowing dagger up, leaned back, and flicked the whip around her enemy's throat. The squid-headed being dropped their sword, both hands grasping at their neck. The hook dug into the creature's flesh, a spurt of greenish ichor flying across the mushy deck.

"You're hurting yourself," Kitty said, "you don't even know it. So many of us do this. We're the worst poison we could take, and keep feeding ourselves the toxins we never wanted. I'm done with it. I reject you and deny you. You can die in your own way and time, but I'll no longer feed you energy or anything else."

The words burst from Kitty, surprising her. This alien being had become something inside of her, and she was now denying it any more power over her. With that thought, that idea, the ship shimmered and faded. The orbs popped like soap bubbles, and the being fell through the planks, plummeting into the night.

Kitty followed, free-falling into the darkness below. A

moment of fear and anxiety tickled at her, but she denied it, too, and let herself fall free of its influence.

14. Collider-Scope

Fritz tore through the last fish-man standing, shredding its throat. Dropping to all fours, he turned towards the animatronic horrors and saw Savage dispatching the last of them. A thundering boom overhead made the were-Pomeranian look up.

The looming clouds were breaking up, chunks of gigantic cephalopod parts raining down around him with wet plopping noises. He leapt to the side, dodging a gelatinous glob of the thing in the sky as it splattered on the pavement. The others did the same, Croaker swearing colorfully and Savage blasting bits that came near. Haunt moaned and collapsed to the asphalt in a heap.

Looking up to see if more things were about to crush him, Fritz saw a small, helpless figure tumbling from the firmament. Now, Fritz wasn't a religious man, but he knew a falling angel when he saw one, and that's exactly what he saw above him. Kitty plummeted towards the ground, her arms and legs splayed outward as if to slow her fall, but she wasn't moving.

"Kitty's unconscious!" Fritz yelped. "I've got her!"

Not waiting for anyone to respond, Fritz jumped to the second level of the center tower, then propelled himself into open air. Landing on a chunk of flesh, he pushed off and upward, his eyes on Kitty as she came closer and closer. In moments, he took one more jump and wrapped his arms around the falling woman. The weight was surprising as he thrust one arm under her knees and the other under her shoulders. Then he was falling, holding Kitty. He looked down, searching for something to land on, to catch so they didn't splatter on the ground below.

Twisting, Fritz angled himself to hit a wall. His feet touched the surface, bending to take the impact, and he pushed towards a twisted piece of balcony below them. He bounced off and ricocheted off a massive blob of tentacled flesh, then another wall, and landed on the ground.

Croaker and Savage stood beside the unconscious Haunt, staring at Fritz with wide eyes.

"Well, hell," Croaker growled, one hand on his hips, the other stroking his weapon. "That was impressive, my fuzzy little friend! But we still have work to do. We need to shut down the kaleidoscope."

"I think he means the machine," Savage said, also in a growl. "We need to break the machine that summoned this thing before something else comes through."

These people growl a lot, thought Fritz, *especially since they're not even were-people.*

"Yah," Fritz nodded, gently setting Kitty next to Haunt. "Let's do the thing. What's first, Croaker?"

"Urg," Croaker rolled his eyes and threw his hands up, "we're down two people, leaving me with you and Savage." Croaker knelt gingerly on the ground, groaning and setting his rifle down. "Okay, let's hope nothing comes for these two while we're out, because we're going to need all three of us for this next part. Fritz, stay furry. From my observations, the entire park is set up to draw something from another dimension or reality. This tower is the focus needle, but there are four other points that will need hit. And they have to be done simultaneously or they might backfire and bring in more defenders."

"How the hell are we supposed to do that when there's only three of us?" Savage asked.

"Timers and radios," Croaker shrugged, emptying his pockets and satchels of the dregs of his cobbled-together gear. "I'll build each of us a bomb with a timer. We synchronize them and then head out to plant them. Easy peasy."

"Wait," Fritz said, raising a furry paw-hand. "If there are four points, but only three of us, how are we going to do that?"

"One of us needs to take two, obviously," Savage muttered, fiddling with his cybernetics. "I'll do it. I've done enough wet work and explosives. I'm the most experienced. Croaker doesn't move very fast, so he should get the closest one. That will also allow him to coordinate the attack once he has his set."

"Maybe," Croaker grunted, screwing two pieces together, then tearing a length of duct tape from a roll with his teeth. "But I think Fritz, unencumbered by armor and gear, might be able to move faster. If he's willing to take on the extra risk, that is."

Looking back to the task at hand, Croaker avoided looking at Fritz. Savage stopped fiddling with his needle gun and locked eyes with Fritz, slowly shaking his head no.

Fritz considered the implications. He was fast when fluffy, but Savage had experience. But the man was temperamental and arrogant, weighed down by implants and attitude. Also, Fritz was a face man, built for gathering intelligence and gear, not doing the dirty work. On the other hand, he was faster and probably smarter than the cyborg.

"I think I should be the one who does it," Fritz said. "I'm faster, smarter, and better looking. Besides, one EMP and you go all kooky, where it will take a small army to stop me."

Three minutes later, Fritz was running at top speed with his tongue flopping out the side of his mouth for one of the seven coasters on the edge of the park. Four were set at the northeast, the southeast, the southwest, and the northwest compass points. Croaker had explained that those four needed to be destroyed, a bomb attached to the cars, so it exploded at the apex of the ride. The remaining three coasters were entry points for more creatures if they failed in their mission.

He was heading for the Eradicator, then for the Pile Driver. Savage was assigned Shatter Mountain, and Croaker took the closest one, the Jolly Kaleidoscope. The Fractured Reality, an indoor coaster, the Dark Portal, a horror coaster, and the Mind Bender, which warned of photosensitive riders having issues, were the remaining ones that Croaker said would become doorways to other places and flood this world with invaders if they failed.

The run to the Eradicator was almost fun and Fritz reached it with no problems, other than having to stop once at a holographic park directory to find the right path. He arrived and stared up at the clacking, whirring tracks. Laser webs cut through the tracks and steel sheets slammed down a moment after the train of cars passed a half-dozen places.

Watching the tracks, Fritz figured the best place to set the explosive charge was on the blade closest to the control booth at the top of the ride. That should take out the operator's nest, the track, and a sheet of steel that might take out parts of the ride below it. Fritz liked the feel of the wind in his fur at high speeds, so it shouldn't be an issue.

Waiting for the next pass, when the cars paused for a few seconds at the loading deck before launching into the first loop, he jumped into the rear car. Not having time to buckle in, he jammed one explosive in his jaws, held on with one hand and had the sticky bomb ready in the other. He checked the timer as he hit the first loop. It said five minutes as he gripped the foam brace bar and his feet flew over his head, then slammed back into the seat as it shot up the steep incline leading to the first massive drop. The control booth would be at the top of the second rise.

Fritz could see the entire park as he clacked up the slope

and noticed the otherworldly flashes of light in the three untargeted coasters. He wished Kitty was awake and could cover anything coming out of at least one. Even Haunt could slow things coming out of one. But if wishes were fishes, then were-cats would be happy.

Cresting the peak, Fritz watched the front of the train car plummet down the intense drop, and he suddenly wished he'd buckled in. His feet came off the seat as his car followed the others, his clawed hand sliding on the bar until he was holding on only by his nails. He slammed back down as he hit the next rise. Turning around, he let go and gripped the seat behind him, waiting to see the guillotine of a steel sheet fall.

It came before he was ready, and he threw the explosive clumsily towards the fast-moving metal. It stuck, and he gave a sigh of relief, looking for a quick exit to get to the ground safely. His earpiece crackled and he heard Croaker.

"Mine is done," the old man said, "heading towards Fractured Reality in case anything comes out."

"Mine too," Savage added, "heading for the Dark Portal in case of an incursion."

It was up to Fritz now. He had to get off this crazy ride, get to the Pile Driver and set the explosive, then to the Mind Bender to make sure nothing came through before the explosives shut down the doorways to whatever realms the Professor-Doctor had connected his massive collider to.

The ground zoomed closer as the cars plummeted and Fritz readied his jump, the second explosive still in his mouth. He jumped, an overhead beam brushing his ears, and he hit the ground in a roll. He came to his feet and face planted into an upright support beam. Stars burst into his vision and he shook his head to clear his sight, stumbling in a circle.

Triple vision settled into double vision, then into singular. Mostly. It was enough, and Fritz staggered in a zig-zag path along what he hoped was the shortest route to the Pile Driver. Within a minute, Fritz was running down the outer path, heading for his next target. Glancing at another holographic directory, he spun down a side path and sped up towards his goal, the remaining explosive now in his hand.

A stuttered sound of gunfire came from two different directions, and Fritz slowed for a moment, wondering if Croaker and Savage were engaging the enemy. Picking up speed, he bent into the wind and shot towards the coaster. Leaping across three lanes of twisting barriers for the line, Fritz landed on a railing and threw himself forward.

He dropped into a crouch on the loading platform and looked up at the massive twisting track overhead. The Pile Driver was a maze of sharp twists and turns with massive blocks that constantly threatened to drop on the riders in the cars. Fritz scanned the ride, trying to figure out where the best place was to plant the device he carried. He glanced at the explosive and saw the timer click past the two-minute mark. One hundred and twenty seconds from now it would blow, taking out everything in a fifteen-meter radius.

The control booth was on the other side of the loading platform, but Fritz couldn't be sure if it would break the connection with the perimeter machine that allowed the things from other worlds to enter this one.

"I'm the idea guy, yah?" Fritz asked no one in particular. "And my ideas always work, right? And if I don't do this right, then the beautiful Kitty will die, yah? Oh, and everyone else on the planet too. So, I guess I just go with my gut."

Raising his nose, Fritz sniffed the air, looking for the best place to set the bomb, which now said he had ninety seconds. He needed time to get to a safe distance and run to the Jolly Kaleidoscope to stop anything that broke through up to the time the connection was severed. The scent in the air told him to shut down the control booth and hope it broke the connection with the track on the loading platform.

"Augh!" Fritz growled. "This wasn't something covered

in anything, ever! To hell with it all, I will do all the things!"

He threw the sticky bomb at the enclosure of the control booth, turning and sprinting away as it hit the glass. He leapt from railing to railing, turning towards the seventh coaster, which was still unguarded. Hitting the asphalt outside of the ride, he sprinted towards the last location under his mission.

The explosion from behind threw him forward, tumbling him heels over head in a multiple somersault. He regained his feet and kept running, not looking back to see if it worked.

"Either," he panted aloud, "it did, or it didn't. Either way, I need to go…"

Fritz went quiet when he saw the entry to the Jolly Kaleidoscope, purplish creatures twice his height flooding through the exit gate and heading towards the central tower where Kitty lay unconscious. Blood-rage flooded him, turning his normally clear and logical mind into a red haze.

"Hey, you okay?" Fritz felt a hand on his midsection shaking him. "Come on, big guy, come back to us."

Fritz's leg spasmed at the sound of Kitty's voice, kicking at the air as the hand kept rubbing his belly. His fuzzy lips curled back in a smile and he felt his red rocket begin to…

"What?" Fritz said, sitting up with a jerk, his hand covering his groin. "Did we win?"

"Yeah," Kitty said, "and you took out a lot of weird looking fragging things. Savage did okay, and Croaker took out a bunch as he guarded me and Haunt."

At the last comment, her voice fell, and she bowed her head, flushing in embarrassment.

"Okay," Savage said, "make out and let's go. The T.A.L.O.N. Agency is at the gates and prepping for a full invasion spree. Let them get in here and clean up."

"I agree with the tin man," Croaker said. "We need to get out of here before we get caught up in their sweep."

"And how the hell do we do that?" Haunt asked, sitting hunched with his elbows on his knees and his head in his hands.

"Jack mentioned," Croaker leaned in, conspiratorially, "that our way home mirrors the real world. So, let's head towards the house of mirrors."

The five gathered themselves and, leaning on one another, made their way towards the holographic hall of mirrors. Croaker was slimmer without all his gadgets and gizmos crammed into his satchel and coat. The older man bent, retrieving bits of electronics and machinery, refilling his pockets along the way. Fritz was half naked and not nearly as furry as he'd been not too long ago. Savage was even too exhausted to complain as he supported the tattered Haunt into the attraction. Kitty followed behind the group, guarding their retreat, but also tossing subtle glances at Fritz's bottom cupped by the orange speedo.

15. Epilogue

Croaker stumbled through the door and into the brightly lit interior of the Traveller's Inn. He carried his satchel in his arms, overflowing with mechanical parts and pieces. Jamie shoved in behind him, pushing past the older man and into the common room. Byron stomped through the door, slapping his hand against the side of his head as if he was attempting to clean water from his ear. Fritz was beside him, wearing nothing but a speedo and a smile. Kitty staggered between the two men, leaning on both of them and looking like she'd been through the ringer.

The cyber-rave look of the tavern was washed out with every light in the room on. It gave the club atmosphere an alien feel like any dark-themed place or warehouse space had when lit up like high noon. Most of the booths were now bare wooden benches and tables, and the dance floor had lost its shine. Everyone in the place turned to look at the returning group, taking in their bedraggled appearances.

"They smell like…low tide!" Tilbert exclaimed, his fingers flying across his hovering keyboard. "Though I guess that's understandable, considering their last encounter."

"Oh, I think there's an added hint of sulphur and ozone

from the explosions and machinery they faced." Elementius studied the group, lowering his glasses perched on his nose to get a better look. "And they're injured. How jolly and exciting. You're getting all this, aren't you, Tilbert?"

"Yes, sir," the student scribe nodded.

"Where the hell is Jack?" Croaker grumbled, looking around and moving to his regular stool at the bar. "And Wanderly is missing also? And Nomed? What's going on here?"

"Why did you bring them with you?" Darome asked, pointing at Fritz, Jamie, and Byron. "Is that allowed? Usually the extras don't come home with the regulars."

"Nuh-uh," Durg rumbled. He pointed at two tables where others sat. "What about Mogits and Manx? And Sam and Tiffene? They all come back with all the others after they did a thing. Then we keep some, and let others go back to where they come from."

"That's true, Durg." Darome beamed at his behemoth companion. "Good eye, you're very smart!"

The half-ogre beamed at the praise, shuffling in place.

Kitty settled onto a stool beside Croaker, and the others joined them.

"Good evening, sir," Cogsley drawled in his overly-proper manner, sliding a bourbon in front of Croaker and a fruity drink to Kitty. "Drinks for each of you?"

"Yeah," Croaker nodded, throwing back his drink. "And another for me. A triple, if you would. And where's Jack, Nomed, and Wanderly? You in charge while they're gone, Cogsley?"

"Perhaps," the automaton said dryly. "But let us take care of our new patrons first, then we can discuss what has transpired while you were away. What can I get each of you?"

The automaton directed the question toward Byron, Jamie, and Fritz. Each ordered a drink, Fritz asking for food, as well. All five echoed his order, and in a few minutes, they were set up with chips, burgers, drinks, and hot towels to clean up.

"Great, we're settled." Croaker looked up and down the bar to show he knew he was right. "Now, stop stalling, you tin can, and tell me what the hell happened here. Where are they?"

"They went to the basement, sir," Cogsley said stiffly, wiping a dribble of ketchup from the bar top beside Jamie. "Wanderly first, then Jack and Nomed followed shortly after."

"This place has a basement?" Kitty asked around a mouthful of food.

"Why is that so surprising?" Jamie looked up from his plate. "Don't most places have basements in them? Is this something weird?"

"It is here," Croaker said. "Cogsley, where's the décor? Why is the bar slowly turning from polished metal to old wood planks? When I sat down, my stool was metal and pleather and bolted to the floor. Now it's a rickety wooden three-legged thing with a V-shaped back."

"Indeed, sir," Cogsley said slowly, turning to take in the changes. "You appear to be correct. It appears the facilities are returning to their original state before Jack took charge."

Professor Elementius and Tilbert crowded to the bar, squeezing in between Darome and the newcomers. The four who'd been sitting at the tables came over to stand behind everyone else.

"Come on, people!" Croaker shouted, flailing his arms around him to clear some space between himself and the people next to him. "You have an entire…"

Trailing off as he turned to point at the rest of the common room, Croaker finished with a small gurgle of surprise. "What the hell happened to the rest of the place?"

"It disappeared," a skinny, middle-aged man with thinning hair said. "Damndest thing, sir. We were just sitting there, minding our own business, when it, well, disappeared."

Everyone stared at the area outside of the bar. What had

been a warehouse-sized space moments ago wasn't much larger than triple the bar-area now. A single row of four tables stood between the group and the far wall, which had a waist-high counter with a foot rail below it running the length of the not-so-far wall.

"Is this because Jack is gone?" Kitty asked.

"Is he dead?" asked Darome with wide eyes.

"Are you okay, Cogsley?" Croaker added, waving at the others to quiet down. "Are you changing, or maybe going to revert to a hat rack or something?"

"Sir," Cogsley said, "if I had eyes, I would roll them right now. I am fine, without alteration or regression. The Traveller's Inn is still here, though I believe we are adrift in the phlogiston. I do believe we will need to find Jack—or barring that, Wanderly—to once again anchor us and reinstate the abilities of this establishment."

"Stuck in the phlogiston?" Tiffene chimed in, tilting her head. "As in, we can't leave without stepping into a realm of magical energy?"

"That's what it sounds like, honey," Darome said, eyes still wide as he picked nervously at his lip.

Durg thumped him comfortingly on the shoulder. "Don't worry," the half-ogre rumbled, "I bet we don't die right now."

Croaker raised both hands to quiet everyone again. "Okay, before panic sets in, I think I have a solution. Cogsley, if I understand you correctly, we need a strong-willed person who has some concept of how this place works to keep it limping along. If we have that, then we may be able to use the Inn to find Jack and the others in the basement. Is that correct?"

"That is the crux of our dilemma," Cogsley nodded.

"Well," Croaker pushed to his feet, "I've been coming around for quite a while now, and I think I'm the best candidate for the job. Plus…" Croaker held up a finger to forestall and unwanted feedback, "I brought a few parts back from our adventure. They look like the type of stuff that opens interdimensional apertures. So, I think I'm the best qualified by years of experience, prepared to do something, and because I said so and dare any of you to say differently."

"I agree," Kitty said, jumping from her stool and standing up to her full height. "I've got Croaker's back. Anyone have a problem with him running things until we get Jack and the others back?"

"No," Fritz said, "I don't think I mind that, and I would say that Haunt and Savage won't complain, either. Mister Norge did an excellent job of guiding us through our last mission."

"And we're just here to observe," Elementius chimed in, nudging Tilbert, who nodded.

"We're pretty new here," Mogits shrugged and waved at the three who'd joined him from the tables, "so I don't think any of us have any objections."

"Darome? Durg?" Croaker asked, turning to the gnome and half-ogre.

"You're the boss pro temp, or something like that," Darome giggled. "And good luck with that!"

ABOUT THE AUTHOR

Travis I. Sivart writes Fantasy, Steampunk, Cyberpulp, Social DIY, and more. You can find him live streaming the writing and editing of his latest project from his home in Central Virginia, surrounded by too many cats.

You can find Travis on Amazon, Barnes and Noble, Books-A-Million, and other literary retailers.

The Traveller's Inn

The Traveller's Inn